D0356504

ALSO BY MARY ROBISON

Days

Oh!

Oh!

by Mary Robison

NONPAREIL BOOKS
David R. Godine, Publisher
Boston

This is a Nonpareil Book first published in 1988 by
David R. Godine, Publisher, Inc.
Horticultural Hall
300 Massachusetts Avenue
Boston, Massachusetts 02115

Originally published in 1981 by Alfred A. Knopf, Inc.

A part of this book first appeared as "The Help" in
The New Yorker, in slightly different form.

Library of Congress Cataloging in Publication Data
Robison, Mary.
OH!
(Nonpareil books ; no. 50)
Reprint. Originally published: New York: Knopf, 1981.
I. Title. II. Series: Nonpareil book ; 50.
[PS3568.O317O37 1988] 813'.54 86-46251
ISBN 0-87923-675-2

First printing
Printed in the United States of America

With affection for the Cennamo kids,

Judy, Teresa, Arthur, Louis, Tommy,

Michael, *and* Donald

Oh!

One

1

A thunderous noise shook the ground and jolted Maureen from her dream. She shoved herself up onto her elbows in grass clippings that whirled like gnat swarms, and looked into the skis of a helicopter bobbing, nose down, yards above her own nose. Noise pressed on the bulb of her skull. She rolled out of her sleeping bag, stood too fast for balance, flumped to her knees. Above her the machine swung like something on the end of a derrick. The man in the Plexiglas bubble wore a headset, had the lenses of his black glasses trained right on her. She scrambled for the patio. The helicopter dipped and chased her, the wash that shot from its blades beating against a row of hedges. She went under the patio's slatted roof. The helicopter, hovering, gave off a siren sound that never got going, a pleading meant just for her.

2

"I'll need a ton of things if you want me to do this right," Lola said. She pressed her hands on her waist, a pretty, brown-skinned woman in her middle thirties. "Rug shampoo, more steel wool, cleanser, a new mop. I'm not going to clean floors with a sponge."

"Sit down, darlin'," Mr. Cleveland said. "We'll hash it out."

"I don't want to sit down. I want to get rolling on the cleaning so I can get it done with," Lola said. She moved from the kitchen doorway into the tile-floored breakfast room, where Mr. Cleveland sat over plates of melon, cuts of fried ham, eggs, and buttered muffins.

He pinned a thick disc of meat with his fork and knifed off a bite. He was fifty-seven, a Texan long ago turned loose on the Midwest. There was a fleshy knob for the end of his nose. He wore a drowsy look and an old-fashioned dressing gown with padded shoulders and wide velvet lapels. He ground the bite of ham with his teeth. "Anyhow, I thought a cleaning person was responsible for furnishing her own tools of the trade."

"I'm not a cleaning person. I'm a cook and a maid," Lola said. "And a valet and a bartender and nurse."

"You have Howdy drive you to the Skyway and charge up whatever you need," Mr. Cleveland said. "Only don't charge an electric garage-door opener or a rotisserie barbecue grill. No drill bits, either."

"No drill bits," Lola said.

Mr. Cleveland quit feeding himself and rested his knife and fork. He poured and drank coffee from a china service.

"Have some coffee," he said.

Lola had begun clearing the plates.

"We've got the whole day to work," he said.

Cleveland was retired, but still had controlling interest in the Whistle-Low Corporation, a company with land holdings and plants that bottled and marketed eighteen varieties of soda pop. The company owned quick-shop food stores, franchised miniature-golf layouts, and even ran a chemistry laboratory. Cleveland had a huge home on a road called Charity Way, a road that wound through a little wood on the border of a country club.

7

"Look what's up from the dead," Lola said.

Howdy came into the breakfast room through the side of the house. He was a tall young man with a big jaw, rusty hair like his father's, and clear blue eyes under white lashes.

"Walk on your shoe toes," Cleveland said to his son. "Lola's puffed up and on a human-rights campaign."

"Morning, Lola," Howdy said.

"That's Miz Turtlidge," Cleveland said.

"Coffee's ready here," Lola said.

"Where's your sister this morning?" Cleveland asked Howdy, who poured coffee, sat down across from his father, and stared sleepily at the vase of day lilies in the middle of the table.

"She slept in the yard again," Howdy said. He scratched at a rough place on his unshaved jaw. "And I hope she stays out there. She's in hysterics. Claims a helicopter dive-bombed her. Oh, and Lola, you're supposed to let Violet stay asleep."

Violet was Maureen's eight-year-old.

"How?" Lola said. She squinted at Howdy.

He picked up and bit into a muffin. "Beats the hell out of me. I'm just relaying the message." He washed down the muffin with coffee and took up another muffin. "Mother used to have a high tea every afternoon," he said. "She'd have muffins like this, and chocolates and biscuits. What you'd call cookies."

"No, I wouldn't," Lola said.

"You can't remember that," Cleveland said. "What your mother would have is a gin fizz and a Hershey bar."

"You hear that?" Lola said.

"Damn teeth," Cleveland said, forkful of eggs in midair.

"Aw," Lola said.

"Aspirin," Cleveland demanded, dropping the fork.

"Aspirin is horrible for your stomach," Howdy said and yawned.

"Grinds it all to hell," Lola said.

"Dr. Lola and Dr. Howdy," Cleveland said.

"Right," Lola said. She brought a swatch of cloth from the

smock she wore over her Levi's and began dusting the leaves of an enormous potted palm that stood in a cement urn before the diamond-paned windows.

Cleveland said, "You're fired, Lola."

"Good," Lola said. "Now I don't have to fix your filthy house."

"I'll hire you back," Howdy said. "At least long enough to get me some of those eggs."

"He'll pay you in canvas," Cleveland said. "An original Howdy every month, twelve naked people a year."

Howdy and Lola were both going to the university. Howdy wanted to be a painter. The carriage apartment where he lived over the old garage was decorated with his acrylic paintings, and so were his shirts and trousers and sneakers. He told people he wanted to be a billboard painter. "No one looks at fine art any more," he'd say, "but everybody looks at billboards."

Lola was headed for the kitchen, carrying the serving skillet. "I'm cleaning," she said. "In the egg and aspirin departments, you can both forage for yourselves."

3

Cleveland struggled with a chain saw as he made his way down the sloped lawn toward his daughter.

"You won't believe something!" she called to him, hands cupped to her mouth.

"Chopper?" Cleveland said. "Just traffic guys, Mo."

"I bet it was Chris," Maureen said.

"Oh, hell, Maureen, no Chris I know flies around with any patrol unit." Cleveland put down the chain saw and sat on his heels. Maureen was cleaning up her campsite from the night before. She had rolled and tied her sleeping bag, piled her magazines, brushed her cigarette butts into a heap, buttoned the leather case over her huge transistor radio, and was collecting her bottles of nail polish and emery boards, stowing them in a box.

"I didn't sleep all night," she said, "and then I'd just dropped off when this helicopter comes swooping down and starts coming at me."

"You're nervous because you've got Chris on the brain," Cleveland said. "Because Chris is on the way, you've got Chris on the brain. You pulled the chopper over with your p.j.'s. Or maybe they were looking for somebody."

Maureen tugged at her pajama top, tried to get it to cover her better, and then, with one finger, she drove her eyeglasses up high on her nose. "Idiot Chris. I hate him," she said.

"Are you calmed down?" Cleveland said. He cleared some sweat from his eye with the palm of his work glove. "It was just a low pass by a helicopter, that's all. It shook me up too."

"Do you believe me that Chris caused it?"

"What I believe is you dreamed the Chris part," Cleveland said.

Maureen was searching the grass around her bare feet. She bent and picked up a matchbook and a loose cigarette, and prepared to light it.

"I just filled this with gasoline," Cleveland said. He hefted the chain saw, jiggled it to make a sloshing noise.

Maureen took the cigarette down from her mouth. "So *that's* what I smell. I thought you had bourbon on your breath already."

"I wish I could have some bourbon," Cleveland said. "I've got a toothache."

"It can't be good to run a saw this early. Especially not with a toothache."

"Early?" Cleveland said. "Honey, it's ten o'clock."

"Oh, hell," Maureen said. "Poor Violet. I gave her strict orders not to leave her room today until I came for her."

Oh!

An amplified guitar sounded a C chord. Cleveland said, "Now just relax. That's nothing but Howdy in the garage."

"I know it is, Father. I'm okay," Maureen said. She walked past him, through the shadow of a beech tree, and up the lawn.

He called after her, "That's just your brother and his friends and their band!"

Maureen was scraping a match. She couldn't get enough friction for a spark.

"They're going to rehearse some," Cleveland said, trailing her. "So you'll know if you hear a lot of ugly noises."

"Daddy, get away from me with that saw," Maureen said. She used the tip of her thumb to mash the head of the match against the striker, then ripped it sideways. A flame blew between her cupped hands.

She was twenty-four, a thin woman with tiny breasts, close-cropped hair, and big ears. Her hair was wavy, bleached almost white. She wore a pair of boy's horn-rimmed glasses.

"I hope you're on your way to see your little girl," Cleveland said. "I hope that's where you're going."

"That's my next stop," Maureen said.

Cleveland went to an old dogwood tree. He snapped the starter rope on his chain saw. He moved carefully around the tree, stooping to nick off the lower branches. Shavings exploded each time the saw touched wood. Maureen worked at her cigarette and stood off on the lawn, watching.

Howdy came slamming out the back door of the garage. He marched toward his father, yelling. But Cleveland wouldn't stop the saw. Howdy turned, exasperated, to Maureen. Both made megaphones with their hands and shouted at their father.

Cleveland cut off the engine and pushed his safety goggles up onto his forehead.

"Why are you doing that *now*? What's *wrong* with you?" Howdy was screaming. "We're trying to rehearse!"

From inside the garage, electric feedback squealed. Someone was beating little riffs on a drum kit, making fluffing noises.

A girl with heavy, big-heeled boots leaned from the garage doorway. She pushed two fingers into her mouth and whistled.

"Eat it, Signoracci!" Howdy shouted.

"Everybody, take it easy," Cleveland said. "Almost done." He leaned over and began bunching the snipped limbs.

The girl whistled again. Howdy said, "I hate this group. I really do. Bunch of kids."

"Then maybe you could keep them out of the house," Cleveland said. "Maybe you could keep them out of Lola's way and out of my beer, and maybe you could tell them to park their van on the drive and not in my rose bushes."

"They didn't," Howdy said.

Cleveland sighed and regarded his daughter. "You going to see about Violet or what?"

"Quit carping," Maureen said.

"Violet and Lola are having a fight," Howdy said.

Blurry guitar noise came splattering from the garage and a single bass note thumped mightily. Maureen put her hand on her chest to see if something was rattling inside.

"I want to make sure you're done with that saw," Howdy said.

"Well, I am," Cleveland said. "For the moment."

Maureen went on up to the casement windows that showed through to the kitchen and breakfast room. She saw Lola standing with her bottom against the stove, her arms tightly folded.

"Your daughter," Lola said when Maureen stepped inside. "I hope you got some fresh air last night and a nice suntan because while you were out, your daughter—"

"Where is she?"

"Locked up," Lola said.

Maureen drove the end of her cigarette into a saucer on the counter. "Fine. Has she eaten anything?" The kitchen still smelled of ham and eggs and coffee.

From the garage, the musicians began a tinny, hammering noise, and Howdy sang, "If . . . I say . . . if . . ."

"Oh, Howdy, shut up," Lola said.

"Really," Maureen said.

Lola went over and closed the windows. "You better come with me," she said.

Violet's bedroom was a mess. The giraffe wallpaper had crayon scribbling all over it. The canopied bed was jammed in a corner, the ruffled flounce in shreds, the outer bed rail wired with a splint. A plastic toy chest molded into the shape of a frog stood with bulging eyes on a throw rug made of fake panda fur.

Violet was in the toy chest sitting in the frog's mouth. "Mom, you said last night I could make breakfast."

"Breakfast is a thing of the past," Lola said.

"I'm sorry," Maureen said. "It's all my fault."

"I was waiting for you to get me up," Violet said, "and you never did."

"You were awake all last night," Lola said. "Don't think I didn't hear you going like mad in here long after the TV signed off."

"I know it," Violet said.

"You were in here playing your records and singing and monkeying around like a crazy person," Lola said.

"I couldn't get to sleep," Violet said.

"It's *my* doing," Maureen said.

"The reason you can't sleep is because you don't get up in the morning. And that's the reason you don't get your breakfast, either," Lola said.

"It's my fault," Maureen said. "I'll fix something quick and I'll be careful not to make any mess."

Violet said, "*I'll* fix it."

"Then neither of you will be hungry for lunch," Lola said. "Just like yesterday and the day before that. So then I've got to fix a second lunch and a second supper and go insane just like the rest of you."

"Okay," Maureen said. "Don't do a thing for us today. Tomorrow, I promise, we'll get up at sunrise or whenever we're supposed to. I'm sorry about today. Today's ruined, so let's forget it." She tried to pick up Violet. But Violet twisted away and ran out the door.

"Violet Ann Cleveland!" Lola called after her. "Come back here instantly."

Violet dragged herself back into the room and bellyflopped onto the bed.

Lola narrowed her eyes. "Go on, tell her," Lola said.

"Go on and tell her what?" Maureen said.

"Tell her what we agreed to tell her. Tell her about the new rules. And don't make me the v-i-l-l-a-i-n."

"Right. Of course," Maureen said. "Let's see."

While Maureen was thinking, Violet melted down the side of the bed until most of her was on the floor.

"Let's see," Maureen said. "Lola works hard here for Grandpa and she has many jobs and *all* of them are very hard."

"And she lives here," Violet said, sliding.

"Yeah," Maureen said, "that's part of the deal."

"Some deal," Lola said.

"But Grandpa does not pay Lola to be your mother or to watch you all day."

"He's not rich enough for that. Nobody is," Lola said.

"Then don't have Lola watch me," Violet said.

"That's impossible," Lola said.

"That's impossible," Maureen said, "when you're always underfoot and asking questions and demanding things. Food and things."

Violet got to her feet, walked purposefully to her portable phonograph, and squatted down in front of it.

"You remember when I made you watch little Boris Schuster?" Maureen said.

"Oh, God," Violet said. She sat up on her knees and began to go through some records piled by the phonograph.

"Well, you see?" Maureen said. "So that's why we have some new rules around here, and you're going to abide by them or else."

Violet lowered a record onto the turntable. She put the tone arm down and eerie organ music came out the tiny speaker. "*Watch out*!" said a man's voice on the record.

"She's not even listening," Lola said.

Maureen kicked the phonograph. It squawked as the needle raked across the record. A bolt of pain raced from Maureen's toes up her shin, and she kicked the phonograph a second time and knocked it on its end. "Damn it, Violet!" she said. "Honey, we were talking to you!"

Violet started, her mouth open.

"You should listen!" Maureen said. She looked at her foot, saw the nail of her big toe bright with blood.

"That was dumb," Lola said.

"Shut up," Maureen said.

"Don't hurt my ghost record," Violet said.

"It'll be fine," Lola said. "If it's not, we'll get you another one."

Maureen limped to the bed, crossed her ankle on her knee, and watched the blood come out.

"I'll get you something for that," Lola said. "If you'll try not to injure yourselves while I'm gone." She walked away down the hall.

"See what happens when a person gets mad?" Maureen said. "Oh, my gosh. Hurt, hurt." She rocked her foot back and forth.

"I'm sorry," Violet said. She got up, wiped her face with the front of her T-shirt, and came close enough to look.

"See?" Maureen said. "This is what happens."

4

Violet was sitting on top of the dishwasher, where Maureen had lifted and deposited her. The kitchen cabinets shook with the vibrations from the bass patterns thundering in the garage. The flatware trembled in the drawers.

"No running ever for anything in the house," Maureen said. "If you've got a question or a problem, hunt me up and don't ask Lola." Using her heel to walk, Maureen was putting together a plate of food for them to share. "You call this brunch," she said.

Violet swung her legs and banged the backs of her Nikes on the dishwasher door.

"All right," Maureen said, and Violet stopped. "Watch what I do here, so you'll be able to do it for yourself sometime." She sliced a tomato in half.

"*Dad*!" Violet screamed.

Maureen dropped the knife and hobbled to the windows.

On the long driveway, where it curved between stands of barbered shrubs, Chris's low-slung import, with its crushed grille and splintered headlight, was moving toward the house.

Violet flung herself from the dishwasher and flew out the back door.

Maureen limped after her. Somewhere along the way she passed the Signoracci girl, a guitar buckled high on her chest, and Howdy, leaning back into the electric roar with his eyes slammed shut and a microphone squeezed in his fist.

Chris stopped his car on the turnaround behind the music makers' van. He sprang from the door and threw himself face down onto the blacktop, arms and legs spread.

"Don't, Dad!" Violet squealed.

Chris got up. He lifted the little girl and cradled her in his bent arm.

"I love you," Violet said.

"Put her down," Maureen said.

"What's your trouble?" Chris said.

"Nothing. Now put her down."

"Come on, Mom," Violet said, wriggling in her father's arm. She reached for the ground with one foot.

Chris set Violet down and propped his hands on her small shoulders. "I'm all through with Canada," he said.

Maureen said, "I saw your helicopter this morning." She grabbed for Violet, who had stepped away from Chris and was pulling at the waistband of her shorts, hiking them up higher on her skinny body.

"Is she nuts? What helicopter?" Chris asked Violet.

"When did you get back?" Maureen said.

"Right now, this minute. I drove straight through. I drove the last hour without a cigarette." He took a look around. "Place is the same." He examined Maureen. "What'd you do, bite your toe?"

"My ghost record," Violet said. "She kicked it."

"Sounds like your mom," Chris said. "She also forgot to wear trousers today."

Violet said, "She's got a swimming suit on underneath her shirt."

"*My* shirt," Chris said.

"You're not allowed here," Maureen said. "Your presence here is unlawful."

Chris frowned, rolled his eyes at Violet.

"I don't care if she hears," Maureen said.

"I'd like a cigarette," Chris said. "Offer me one and I'll tell you about my trip. It's a story."

"Not interested," Maureen said. Behind her, the drummer began batting out a tumbling solo routine.

Chris hunkered down in front of Violet. He closed his eyes and snapped his fingers completely out of time with the music.

"Dad?" Violet said. "Quit doing that." She put her hands on his face. "Da-ad. I never got my breakfast and Lola wouldn't feed me."

"Who's Lola?" Chris said.

"Lola," Maureen said.

"Oh, *Lola,*" Chris said, winking broadly at Violet.

"You better have a good reason for showing up here," Maureen said.

Chris stood up, his jaw muscles bunching behind his flared nostrils. "You better change your tone with me. I've been awake a long time." He was ten years older than Maureen, a sharp, good-looking face—all angles—longish, fair hair.

Maureen pawed her shirt pocket for a cigarette. She found one and handed it to Violet, who passed it on to Chris. "You better not hurt anybody," Maureen said.

"Why would I hurt anybody?" Chris said. He bit off the filter, slapped his pockets for a match. He took the cigarette from his lips, rolled it between his fingers. Tobacco fell out. "Defective," he said, and snapped the cigarette at Maureen's legs.

The girl guitarist stalked out of the garage, striking her instrument. Her lips popped each time her guitar rang. She threw her leg over the extension cord that was drawing taut behind her, and spun on the heel of her jackboot. Chris laughed and tossed his head.

Cleveland came around from the side of the garage. He put down the rake he was carrying and looked at Chris. "So, how're you doing?" Cleveland said, and shook Chris's hand.

"Good," Chris said. "Really good."

"Yeah, well, I'm just here piddling around with the yard," Cleveland said.

"It looks a little baked," Chris said.

"Oh, sure, it's parched," Cleveland said. "It's burnt but not for lack of water or the heat or anything. It's that Lawn Dinner or whatever they call it. Never should have put it down."

"No?" Chris said.

Cleveland leaned a little to one side and spat. "No."

"The bushes are looking nice," Chris said. He stood with his feet apart and his arms folded.

"Yeah, and my primroses are in great shape," Cleveland said. "Cherry trees are fine, so are the roses. Everything that didn't get burned to the ground by the Lawn Dinner is fine."

"Lotta work," Chris said. He leaned over and spat too.

"Oh, it's work," Cleveland said.

"Who put down the fertilizer?" Chris said. "You or your gardener?"

"Guilty as charged," Cleveland said, and raised his hands as if surrendering to guns. "So when did you come back from Canada or wherever you were, Chris?"

"Just this second. Interstate all the way from the border."

"That's the route," Cleveland said.

"He won't leave," Maureen said.

"You want him to leave?" Cleveland said. He pulled a handkerchief from his shirt pocket and bent his neck to blow his nose. "What are you, in a motel, Chris? You visiting or did you come back to live?"

"I'll get a room near campus. There's this house I know of," Chris said. He was scrubbing a little area of the drive with the toe of his shoe. "It's a room for students, like, and all the students are gone for the summer. I'll get it cheap."

"So you'll live down on campus," Cleveland said.

"Week to week," Chris said.

"What are you doing for a job?" Cleveland said. "Or do you have any? I hope you didn't spend all your lottery money."

"No," Chris said.

"You didn't blow the whole one hundred G's on a new car, I see," Cleveland said.

"No, sir," Chris said, still scuffing the pebbles in the driveway. "But the money was two years ago, just about. So I work, on and off, for the hell of it. Hang drywall or something. Carpentry. It keeps me tan."

Signoracci's guitar noise flared up again, but abruptly stopped. The bass and drums continued a moment, then dribbled out.

Howdy came out of the garage. He had a black bullwhip

curled in one hand. "Breakdown!" he called to them. "The wattage blew our amp."

"Good work," Cleveland said.

"You don't go for Howdy's group?" Chris said, grinning.

Cleveland looked at him sideways, then shut his eyes.

Howdy angled, barefoot, off the hot blacktop for the grass.

Signoracci continued fingering the neck of her guitar, but no sound came from it. She talked to herself as she pressed and picked the wires.

"That one's far gone," Cleveland said.

Violet padded over to Howdy and tried to snatch his whip away from him, but Howdy held it high.

"I was leaving," Chris said. "But I'd like to see this first, whatever it is."

"Whip stunts," Cleveland said. "Stick around."

"Thanks," Maureen said.

"Stand back, Violet," Howdy warned.

Violet backed up a little. She put both her arms into her shorts up to the elbows. She bent over at the waist.

Howdy shook out the bullwhip and walked backward on the lawn, turning and flicking his wrist in front of him so that the length of plaited leather swept the grass and doubled back on itself.

"Violet, get back!" Maureen shouted. "Your Uncle Howdy is doing something dangerous!"

"On the news," Cleveland said to Chris, "I saw this report about a guy in Hollywood who can take a snake whip and untie the knots in ladies' halters. You ever see that?"

Chris, who had propped himself against the side of his car, shook his head.

Howdy began winding the whip in the air. He drew his arm down sharply. The whip buckled, made a soft pop. Howdy cursed. He tried again, whirling the leather until it whistled, then cut his arm down with a jerk.

The whip made a splashing noise.

"Give me that thing!" Chris shouted.

"Stay put!" Howdy yelled back.

"Come on!" Chris yelled. "Give it here before you do yourself harm!"

"No!" Howdy shouted.

Chris started across the lawn.

Cleveland clasped his hands behind his head and chewed the inside of his cheek.

Maureen took Violet inside, and pushed her into one of the captain's chairs that ringed the breakfast table. "Now," Maureen said, "food."

She set out bowls, drinking glasses decorated with Tweetie Pie the canary and Sylvester the cat. For napkins, she folded two sections of paper towels.

"Can't I go outside and eat?" Violet said. "I want to watch what Dad's doing."

"He's not your dad, Violet. I've told you that a thousand times. You don't have a dad."

"Really?" Violet said.

"Really," Maureen said.

Outside, something cracked like rifle fire. Maureen went to the bank of windows. She stood there, gazing through the leaves of English ivy that hung in baskets above the casements.

She saw Cleveland crouched over, helping the Signoracci girl with the socket on her guitar. She saw Howdy staring. She saw Chris in the turnaround working the whip. He swatted it, making crisp zigzags that ended in fierce, smacking explosions.

5

Howdy was driving Lola to the Skyway in his MG. They were on the way to get her cleaning supplies. He had taken a shortcut down a graveled road, speeding along, wearing wraparound sunglasses and white, perforated gloves. "My mother did paintings!" he shouted at Lola. "She won some prizes at county fairs! Landscapes!"

Lola was gripping her seat and the door of the rattling MG. They bucketed over a pothole.

"She was Irish and very moody! Her pictures are typically Irish! It was always raining and there were no people in them!"

"Maybe she couldn't draw people!" Lola screamed.

"Maybe!" Howdy shouted. "Anyway, she divorced Daddy and went back to Dublin! I was ten! Maureen was six!"

"You told me! Your father told me too!" Lola screamed. "Could you slow down, do you think?"

"Don't think about it!" Howdy shouted. He twisted the wheel, and the car veered around a broken liquor bottle. "How're your classes?"

"Not good! I don't have time to do the reading!"

"What?"

"The *reading*! It's slow going. I don't have time to concentrate!"

"Yeah! Me too! One thing I found out, though! I don't want to be a painter any more! That's all a racket and you have to kiss somebody's behind to have your work looked at! I think I'm through with rock bands too! Because of the people! But guess what!"

"Can't guess!" Lola screamed.

"I took a drama class as an elective!"

"Uh-oh," Lola said.

"For my first project, I did Tom's opening speech from *The Glass Menagerie*! I got an A-plus!"

"They don't have those plus-jobs in the Humanities Department!" Lola screamed.

"Don't tell Daddy, but I also painted the scenery for the summer fête! It's a musical, night after tomorrow! I'm in the chorus!"

"You'll *sing* in it?" Lola screamed.

Howdy worked the clutch and yanked the gearshift for a

sharp corner. "It's a reworking of an ancient tragedy, and we put in tunes!"

"That's nice!" Lola screamed.

"I really think I was born for the stage!" Howdy screamed back.

6

The Skyway was a discount store, larger than an aircraft hangar and newly constructed on acreage that had been graded from corn fields. There seemed to be three square miles of parking space sectioned by concrete islands and curbs and by ropes hung with colored flags. Toward the back of the lot, floating among the parked cars, was one of Cleveland's miniature-golf courses. It specialized in Oriental-looking props and chartreuse-carpeted runways.

A teenager in blue makeup and an orange wig stood in front of Skyway's stream of automatic doors. He was hawking helium balloons stamped with pictures of footwear.

Lola got a shopping cart and trundled it up and down the wide aisles of sporting goods, toys, cameras, fabrics, pyramids of cut-rate motor oil. Howdy tagged after her, singing along with the Muzak.

"Settle down," Lola said.

Howdy went off to inspect the art supplies while Lola rolled the cart around the housewares department filling up the basket. When she had everything she wanted, she pushed up to the checkout counters and stood waiting for Howdy because Howdy had the charge card.

After twenty minutes, she left the cart and went to hunt for him. First she tried the groceries section of the store, where the air conditioning was so powerful the employees wore sweaters. Then she tried the notions section, asking a lady who sat behind a tiny desk if she had seen anyone who looked like Howdy.

"No, honey," the lady said, "but let me get those sunglasses clean for you." Lola gave the woman her glasses, and watched while they were coated with a slimy fluid and then rubbed dry with a terry-cloth towel.

"Breathe on them," the lady said, handing the glasses back to Lola. "With C-Kleer, they won't steam up."

Lola tried to fog her glasses with her breath. She couldn't. She bought two tubes of C-Kleer.

She searched through the clothing section, and there he was, in men's sportswear, posing in front of a triptych of mirrors in a white paratrooper's jump suit, high-topped sneakers, and a scarlet ascot.

"I was about to report a lost child," Lola said.

"Ray?" Howdy said. "This is Lola." Howdy introduced the chunky salesman standing beside him. "This is Ray," Howdy said, and the salesman nodded.

"Don't you love this coverall?" Ray said.

"What are all the zippers for?" Lola said.

Ray smiled.

"I can see his underpants through that stuff," Lola said.

"I have complete movement," Howdy said. He did a deep knee-bend.

"I think it's for girls," Lola said. "Can we please go? Buy that dress, and let's go."

"You'll see a lot of these this season," Ray said.

"Don't bring that joke to me on washday," Lola said.

"It's new and it takes getting used to," the salesman said. "I think your wife here will get to like it."

"His wife?" Lola said.

"I'm not pushing the thing," Ray said, "but I had a guy bought two and he was back yesterday to get seven more."

Howdy looked pleased. He did some turns before the mirror. "I'll take it," he said. "And you can bag my old clothes."

7

Cleveland swung his slippered feet down from the davenport. "Great to see you all," he called to Lola and Howdy. "You have a good vacation in Tibet or what?" He had been watching television in the den, drinking a watered Scotch.

"So what's going on here?" Lola said, nodding at the television set.

"Same as yesterday," Cleveland said.

8

Lola wrote out a list of cleaning plans and stashed it in the pocket of her smock. She went upstairs to Maureen's room with a basket of laundered clothes and her new bucket of stuff.

Maureen was sitting on her bed, her short white hair in rollers, her feet drawn up. She was painting dark red lacquer on her toenails, all except the one that was covered with a bandage. The smell of acetone was terrific.

"What's that sound I keep hearing?" Maureen said.

"Your brother's new high-top sneakers," Lola said. "They're in the clothes dryer. He wanted them broken in."

Lola went out of the room for a minute and came back with a bottle of glass cleaner. " 'On only tiny things that tear . . .' " she murmured to herself.

"What?" Maureen said, carefully unhooking her rollers and racking them back in their case.

"Just a minute," Lola said. She stopped in the middle of the room and stared at her shoes.

"Never mind if you don't want to tell me," Maureen said.

"Sure," Lola said. She went to the front window and striped it with cleaning spray. "I'm writing a poem in my head."

Maureen used her fingers to ruffle the stiffness out of her hair. "I didn't know you wrote poetry." She leaned between her parted knees, flexed her toes, and blew on the nails.

"I haven't since high school," Lola said. "This is for my Creative Writing class. The professor told us he didn't want sunsets or sea gulls, and no love junk."

"I'd rather be hit by a school bus than write a love poem," Maureen said.

" 'There are many days and terrible ways, to waste my bitter pride,' " Lola recited. " 'On only tiny things that tear, something, something, something.' "

"That's angry and ugly," Maureen said.

"No, it's *about* anger," Lola said, "and about how we waste it on a million little annoyances instead of on what's really chewing at us." She worked her paper towel around on the window glass. "Professor Riley got on my back last week. He jumped all over me for being black."

"I thought you told me *he* was black." Maureen was busy pinching the bandage on her toe.

"He is. But he says I'm not dealing with the New Negro. He says I don't even know what the New Negro is," Lola said.

"What's your favorite flower?"

"Jonquils," Lola said.

"Then that's it," Maureen said. "That's your topic."

"Not jonquils. Riley says stay away from flowers and children."

"Then Violet's doubly out," Maureen said. She got off the bed and draped herself in a beach towel on which the word *Capri* was scrawled, as if in lipstick, dozens of times.

"More sunbathing?" Lola said.

"Sleep," Maureen said. "I've been trying to find a safe

place to sleep ever since that helicopter came down at me this morning."

"You sleep more than anyone I've ever known," Lola said. "How can you do it so much?"

"It's a gift," Maureen said. She stepped through a small door out onto a little rooftop balcony surrounded by latticed fencing. She stepped back inside. "Goddamn it, Chris is back."

"I didn't know he ever left," Lola said.

They watched Chris. He had gotten himself onto Violet's tiny bicycle, and he pumped across the backyard, standing on the pedals for leverage. The bike inched to the top of a grade. There was a sharp hill all around the yard proper, and Chris shot down it with his feet spinning furiously and then coasted on his momentum to the very back of the house. He tweaked the air horn on the handlebars, and yelled, "Hey! Mo!"

Maureen stepped back from the window.

"Oh, come on!" he yelled. "I see you!"

He let the bike fall and vanished out of view. Maureen and Lola heard banging noises, a loud scrape, and after a while they saw Chris's hands reaching for the latticework fence. He hauled himself up and over, dusted his palms, and removed one of Cleveland's crimson roses from under his belt. He held the flower out to Maureen, who had shut the little glass-paned door and thrown its bolt.

"Who does he think he is?" Lola said. She took one of Maureen's pillows and stuffed it into a laundered pillowcase.

Chris was shouting something, but his words were impossible to hear over Maureen's air conditioner.

"The big child," Maureen said.

Chris smiled through the door. He poked the rose into his mouth, chewed on the petals, and swallowed them.

"You're not funny," Maureen said. She flapped her beach towel. She spread it on the rug beneath her and sat cross-legged. She sighed and, keeping her eyes on Chris, lit a fresh cigarette.

On the balcony, Chris brought a flat brown pint of whiskey from his hip pocket. He took some gulps and, mimicking drunkenness, reeled close to the railing and then leaned dangerously over.

Lola said, "Go ahead and fall." She stood behind Maureen and shook out a clean sheet fragrant with fabric softener.

"We're not that lucky," Maureen said.

Chris charged the door. He pressed his nose against the glass.

"Get lost," Lola yelled.

Maureen crossed the room to tap the ash off her cigarette. "Now you see where Violet gets all that violent energy. I knew it wasn't from me. All I want to do is sleep."

Lola smoothed the top sheet and tucked down the corners.

Maureen was going through her bureau drawer for a comb when she heard Lola gasp. She looked and saw Chris at the balcony door. He had dropped his jeans so that Lola could get a good look at his buttocks.

"Very mature, Chris!" Maureen yelled.

"Isn't that *sickening*?" Lola said, laughing.

Maureen drew on her cigarette. Burning ash flew down and hit her bare leg. "That does it," she said. "These smokes *are* defective."

She went back to the balcony door, yanked open the bolt, and swung the door open. Chris hiked up his pants and struggled to get them snapped.

"Why do you haunt me?" Maureen said. "What pleasure do you find in it? Please tell me, because I'd really love to know."

"Easy," Chris said. He buckled his belt and picked up the pint of whiskey. "I officially consider you my wife."

"The *law* doesn't. No one does."

"*I* do," Chris said. He uncapped the bottle and swigged from it. "You know what I've been thinking?"

"I certainly don't."

"I've been thinking we ought to get married. Once and for all. Yes or no? A simple answer will do."

"Absolutely never."

"Okay," Chris said.

"You're insane," Maureen said.

"I've also been thinking about the kid," Chris said. "I've been wondering a lot about Violet. How can she be happy, living the way she does?"

"Ha!" Lola said.

"Really, Chris," Maureen said. "That's beneath even you."

"To be concerned for my daughter? In this house? You know," Chris said, "very soon now you're going to have to marry me or somebody. I don't think you'll be able to stand it here. You'll have to get out."

"This is interesting," Maureen said. "This is really interesting. I'll have to leave?"

"Yes. I think so. Probably," Chris said. "For one thing, Howdy won't be staying. He's got a girl or something. That leaves your dad and, of course, Lola, and they're both worse than Howdy." He wiped his lips with his bicep, sucked a breath, and tried to look competent. "Everybody knows Violet regards me as her father. Which I am. And insofar as the standards go around here, I've been an excellent father. That's my opinion."

"Insofar as the *standards* go," Maureen said.

Chris weaved a little and braced his back on the railing. "Don't interrupt me, Mo. I'm determined to say this. If you don't get out of here soon, your dad's going to core your apple. You'll go completely and irretrievably off your rocker. It's me or it's him. Only you can decide. There are forces at work here—things closing down. I've felt them, Mo. I really have."

"Are you drunk?" Maureen said. "Because it's okay, if you are. I get drunk."

"It might as well be me that saves you," Chris said.

"I'd prefer somebody with manners," Maureen said.

"I'm the best you're going to get." He drank from the bottle, capped it, and dropped it on the deck of the balcony. He turned and vaulted over the railing.

"Jesus!" Maureen said.

Lola hurried out from the bedroom, and the two women stood leaning over the little fence.

"Some jump," Lola called down.

"Some father," Maureen said.

"That's just an example!" Chris called back to them.

9

The late-afternoon sun was moving the roof's shadow closer to Maureen's *Capri* towel, but the air was still warm enough to bring sweat out under her eyes. The balcony seemed to sway beneath her. She was nearly asleep.

"Mom?" Violet whispered. She came out onto the balcony, a copy of *Countdown* magazine in her hand. She was wearing her Brownie uniform.

Maureen rolled her head and blinked. "Hi, honey."

"Here," Violet said. She held out the magazine.

"Not right now," Maureen said.

Lola said, "Don't tell me I never did anything for you." She had followed Violet upstairs with a glass of beer for Maureen.

"I'm marking it down," Maureen said. "I'm going to put it in the big book."

"Here, Mom. Lookit." Violet showed a page in the magazine. "I drewed this."

"You *drew* it," Lola said.

"You did, Violet?" Maureen said. "It's excellent, honey. It's a beautiful swan."

"Actually, it's not a swan," Lola said.

"It *can* be a swan," Violet said.

"Well, it's an almost perfect drawing," Maureen said. She

lay on her side with her face on her arm and studied the page. "Mommie's so beat," she said.

Violet flopped down on one edge of the towel and lay stiffly on her stomach. She turned her face to Maureen's.

Violet's hair was temporarily blond from the sun. She had orange freckles, permanent. Her shoulders, under her Brownie uniform, were wide and muscled like a little boy's. Her clear gray eyes stayed fixed on Maureen's.

"Cut it out, Violet. You're giving me the creeps."

"Mom? I'm hot."

"Me too, baby," Maureen said. "It's the sunshine."

"Inside I'm hot," Violet said.

"I don't know what you mean, honey."

Violet sighed and went on staring.

"Honestly, Vi, can't you go eyeball someone else?"

"Why don't *you* move?" Lola said. "Sit up and drink your beer."

"Don't want to," Maureen said.

"Well, you've got the whole damn porch," Lola said. "So why are you lying face-to-face on top of each other?"

"I don't know," Maureen said.

The extension phones all over the house rang. Lola went away and came back. "For you," she said to Maureen. "Him."

"We're not here today," Maureen said.

"We are so." Violet said. "It's Dad."

"He's not your dad," Maureen said wearily.

"This morning I told her he is," Lola said. "She always asks me, and I always tell her."

"You have no dad," Maureen said.

Lola sat down beside them. Out on the great lawn, evening was setting in, the bushes and trees turning gray.

"This is just about the time my father would make it home from work," Lola said. "He'd come in hot and growling and mean-headed, and my mom would stay away from him. He'd sit on the sofa and eat what was left in his lunch box—he worked a lathe at Garfield Aircraft—and I'd pester him to read me the paper. Mom would bring him his beer and then she'd disappear. He'd drink it and eat an orange or a sardine sandwich and a pepper from our truck garden. They were the hottest things, those peppers. Nobody could eat them but him."

Violet turned onto her back and began to cry.

"What on earth?" Maureen said.

"Did I say something, Violet Ann?" Lola said.

"This boy I hate," Violet said. "Fritz! He was at the recreation center on the . . . *you* know."

"We *don't* know," Maureen said.

"The tumbling mat and I was playing after my Brownie meeting. And he went and got this, uh, like a mop—and held it up and said, 'This is your hair!' "

"Fritz who?" Lola said.

Maureen said, "That just means he's in love with you, honey. Your hair is perfect. It's the style now to have weatherblown hair."

"I'd say you are in step with the style," Lola said.

"Well, he tore out a lot of my hair," Violet said.

"No, he didn't," Maureen said. "He *pulled* your hair."

"It hurts when they pull it," Lola said. "It feels like it's being yanked out when they do that."

"He showed me a big handful of my hair," Violet said, and sobbed.

"He was playing a trick on you," Maureen said.

"Let's see your head," Lola said. "Sit up."

"No, never mind," Violet said, and sniffed. "He didn't pull out too much."

"Just shrug it off," Maureen said.

"Well, here's where he blasted me with the mop." Violet raised her hem and pointed to a welt on her thigh.

"Was that with the handle? What a drag!" Maureen said.

"What's his last name, Violet? I'll call his father," Lola said.

Maureen said, "Always remember, Violet, that boys are incredibly stupid imbeciles who are liable to do anything to you at any time."

"Why do they?" Violet said.

"Because we girls' prettiness drives them crazy," Maureen said.

"That's right," Lola said.

10

So this is where everyone is," Cleveland said. He was dressed in a cream-colored poplin suit and a tie the hue of shrimp sauce. "Three lazy bugs. I want you all to say hello to Virginia. Come on, Virginia." He led his new lady friend, whom they had all met once before, out into the evening sun. Virginia was a leggy woman. She wore a white cocktail dress. Her yellow-red hair was pinned in a neat chignon.

Lola and Maureen exchanged looks. "Oh my gosh, look at you two," Lola said. "Beautiful!"

"I'll say," Maureen said.

Violet took her beanie from where it was tucked in her uniform belt and chewed absently at its edge.

"Off to the Ritz, I guess," Lola said.

Virginia and Cleveland were laughing and glancing down at their clothes.

"As nice as you look, Dad, this woman is still too good for you," Maureen said.

"That's what she keeps telling me," Cleveland said, and smacked his hands together and rubbed them briskly.

"No place in this town is classy enough for you two. It's a shame," Lola said.

"Everyone can drop the blarney," Virginia said, beaming and red-faced.

"Sweet potato, what's the trouble?" Cleveland said to Violet, who shrugged.

"Nothing, nothing," Maureen said. She shook her head at her father. "It's all taken care of. Really. Handled already."

"If you've got kid problems, talk to Virginia. She's a real kick in the figurative pants along those lines," Cleveland said.

"Oh, I am *not,*" Virginia said. "I've never even had children of my own."

"That's easy—to deal with your own. Your *own* kids, you can kick the hell out of them. But you do something much harder, babycakes," Cleveland said. He appealed to Lola and Maureen. "She does something much harder. Every Sunday morning she takes on a dozen Violet-sized hooligans, and she keeps them happy as clams. And that's with their parents watching."

Virginia was the hostess of a church-sponsored TV show that aired at seven o'clock on Sunday mornings.

"She keeps them handled, all right," Cleveland said.

"We know," Maureen said. "Don't we, Vi? We know all about 'Wonderbox.' "

Violet nodded, looking away.

"You watch 'Wonderbox,' Violet?" Cleveland said. "Do you like it?"

Virginia said, "Oh, leave her alone and don't embarrass the child." But she studied Violet with a hopeful expression.

Lola said, "*I* do."

"It's wonderful," Maureen said, "how Virginia can run that show. Violet and I always watch it."

"Oh, come on, Maureen," Cleveland said. "When was the last time you were out of bed at seven o'clock on a Sunday?"

"Oh, now, now," Virginia said, "Maureen's a little too old for 'Wonderbox.' "

"Is she too old to sleep in a bed?" Cleveland said. "Or live in a house instead of a yard?"

"Settle down," Maureen said.

"Grook," Violet said.

"Violet, that's right!" Cleveland said. "You do watch Virginia's show, don't you? Grook is the clock, who helps us tell time."

"He's good," Lola said.

"I told you we watched," Maureen said.

Cleveland said, "And this here, Violet, is Miss *Virginia.*"

"I know it," Violet said.

"She tells us about the animals, the weather, and God," Cleveland said.

"Violet knows," Maureen said.

"Do you make up that show?" Lola said. "Or does someone write a script? How do you know what the right things are to tell children? You have a specialist or an adviser?"

Virginia smiled. "Oh, now," she said.

"Well, you're doing something right," Maureen said. "You've been on the air quite a while."

"Thirteen years," Virginia said. "And it was thirteen years ago that I was born again. You wouldn't guess I'm only thirteen years old, would you, Violet?"

"Yes," Violet said.

"Isn't that nice," Lola said.

"You joke," Virginia said, "but it's like starting all over. When your sins are washed away, you are born all over again. It'll come to you, Maureen. And you too, Lola. I'm confident it will."

"I sort of have my own religion," Maureen said.

"Sleep," Lola said.

"She believes in being asleep," Cleveland said.

"Can we have supper?" Violet said.

"In a minute," Maureen said. She picked up the glass of beer Lola had brought her and swallowed about half of it.

"Maureen's decided not to eat meat," Cleveland said.

"What a shame," Virginia said. "It's one of the four major food groups."

Down in the yard, in the branches of the saplings, starlings were landing and making noise. A bat careened crazily out over the line of woods.

"Well, I better stir myself," Lola said.

"Can I have supper?" Violet said.

"So where are you two going to, all gussied up?" Maureen said.

"We're not sure. We're narrowing it down," Cleveland said.

"I can't get over how you both look. Especially Virginia," Lola said. She was up and dusting the back of her Levi's with her hands.

Cleveland said, "Lovely. Virginia looks lovely."

"Just like little Violet," Virginia said. "Only Violet doesn't need all the lipstick and the makeup."

"Oh, I don't know," Maureen said. She took another swallow of beer. "Maybe Vi could use a little eyeliner."

"Help me heat the soup," Lola said. She snatched at Violet's hand and led her off the balcony.

"Good night," Violet called.

Virginia waved good-bye, swinging her whole arm in a wide arc. It was the good-bye wave she used on her television show.

Cleveland cleared his throat and walked Virginia the short distance to the balcony railing. Virginia turned her face to the pink sun and leaned on the rail and crossed her thin legs at the ankle.

"Hey," Cleveland said, "I've got a bone to pick with you, Maureen."

Maureen made a great sigh, and then put a wingseed between her teeth and idly chewed its stem. "Oh, really," she said.

"I picked up the phone downstairs, to make reservations somewhere," Cleveland said, "and somebody was already on the line—Chris. He was waiting for you to come to the phone. He'd been waiting, he said, for almost a half hour."

"That's awful," Maureen said.

"You think it's funny to tie up the phones like that? What if an emergency call were trying to get through?"

Maureen gulped the last of her beer, "Give me a for instance of the emergency you're expecting."

"Don't get smart," Cleveland said. "I warn you, I'm pretty mad."

"Settle down," Maureen said.

"You see how she is?" Cleveland said. He turned back to Maureen. "Look, if you don't want to talk to someone, tell him, and get off the damn line in case of an emergency."

"What's all these emergency calls?" Maureen said. "Is this the White House?"

"You're testing me," Cleveland said. "Don't test me."

11

Lola was standing on the kitchen counter, reaching into the top shelf of a high cabinet. The overhead lights snapped on. "You'll ruin your eyes," Cleveland said.

She sat down on the counter, her shoulders slumped with fatigue. "Violet's cooperating so far," she said. "I got her fed and in her room with the portable television."

"That's good," Cleveland said. "That way you can really hit the books tonight. Virginia and I are stepping out soon, so we won't bother you. You got Maureen mooning around on the roof, though. Where's Howdy?"

"I don't know, but there's food," Lola said. "I have food for everybody. It's under foil in the stove."

"Well," Cleveland said, "if the furnace explodes or there's a forest fire, you have Howdy take care of it. Don't consider calling me at the restaurant. If Violet gets taken hostage, or a strangler breaks in and kills Maureen, you're to phone the police. In the event you have an appendicitis attack, let Howdy operate. Don't disturb me for anything except if you've been cut off by army ants."

"Hell, I can handle army ants," Lola said.

"You look beat," Cleveland said. He nodded sympathetically and glanced around the kitchen. "Where'd you hide my Scotch?"

"Cupboard over the trash compactor."

Cleveland mixed two drinks with soda and ice. He said, "Violet's being good for a change?"

"Um hmm. She's an awfully good child." On the counter there was a newspaper opened to the crossword puzzle. Lola took a pencil from her smock and touched it to the tip of her tongue. "Sweetmeats!" she said, and wrote the word in. She looked up at Cleveland. "Maybe you ought to think about going wherever you're going."

"I'm minding the time," Cleveland said.

Virginia came into the kitchen. She had been freshening her makeup in the downstairs bathroom and she was tugging at the bodice of her gown and fingering her pearls as she walked.

"My stars and garters," Cleveland said. He handed Virginia a glass.

She sipped and shook the ice. "Have we decided?"

"My vote is for the Steak Warehouse. They have lots of seating and all kinds of entertainment stuff. It's a converted factory is what it is," Cleveland said. "With a barbershop quartet that strolls around. Mickey Rooney ate there."

"I hear it's terrible," Virginia said.

"The waiters are on roller skates," Cleveland said.

"I'm sold," Lola said. "Too bad I'm not invited."

Virginia said, "I was thinking of the Rue de Lenoire."

"Here's the problem with that," Cleveland said. "We don't have reservations and the food costs a billion dollars and you get enough for a fly on a diet."

"It's very sweet," Virginia said. "It's a tiny, five-star place, with a good wine cellar and foreign waiters with accents. Lenoire, who runs it, is an old friend of mine. You'd swear you were in Europe."

"You'd swear you had your pocket picked," Cleveland said.

"What about Bacon's?" Lola said. "You'd love it there."

"What's Bacon's?" Cleveland said.

"Bacon's is down on Fourth. You've got live music," Lola said. "Hickory-smoked ribs and Texas chili. They give you a bucket of dark beer for only two bucks. I have a friend who used to drive all the way from Pennsylvania just for one of their blue-cheese burgers."

"Sounds quaint," Virginia said.

"They have their own pizza oven," Lola said.

"I think I've heard Howdy talk about this place," Cleveland said. "You feel like an adventure, Gin?"

"Don't I always?" Virginia said.

Maureen came into the kitchen and set down her empty glass. She didn't speak to Cleveland. She smiled tightly at Virginia, and swung open the refrigerator door. She popped the ring tab on a can of beer and drank.

Virginia touched her pearls. "Perhaps we're overdressed, though."

"For Bacon's?" Lola said. "Bacon's gets all types."

"Bacon's!" Maureen said. "Who in the hell is going to Bacon's?"

"We are," Cleveland said. "Why? What's wrong with it?"

"Oh, don't listen to her," Lola said.

Maureen said, "If I were to go up to Howdy's place right now, and put on his oldest clothes, I'd still be overdressed for Bacon's. It's for kids. Virginia wants to eat in a restaurant, don't you, Virginia?"

"I loved the place," Lola said.

"Years ago. It's a real dive."

"Well, Howdy says it's great," Lola said.

Maureen said, "That's because it's the only place in the Midwest that will hire Howdy's band."

"I do like jazz," Virginia said.

"Howdy doesn't play jazz," Maureen said.

"I've got the solution," Cleveland said. "We'll have Lola

and Maureen rustle us up some food here, and then we'll go to Bacon's and drink dark beer."

"They smoke at Bacon's," Maureen said.

"Smoke?" Virginia said.

"Marijuana," Maureen said. "Everyone smokes marijuana at Bacon's."

"Oh, Virginia and I smoked marijuana over at Father Deluka's house," Mr. Cleveland said. "Nothing even happened. That's all in the head."

"You smoked pot?" Maureen said to Virginia.

"Lola's got some food here. We can all make something. Salad or something," Cleveland said.

Lola looked up from her puzzle. "What? Listen, I'm retired for the day. I don't have any food here except this little bit of stuff under foil."

The front-door chimes sounded. Lola sighed and eased down from the counter.

"We'll get it," Maureen said, following Lola out of the kitchen.

"Sit still," Cleveland said, going after them. "*I'll* get it."

They opened the door to a slender, snaggle-toothed girl wearing boy's pants and rawhide work gloves. She was leaning on a shovel. "Howdy in there?" the girl asked.

"Howdy out *there*!" Cleveland said, and chuckled.

"I knew he'd say that," Lola said.

"No, Howdy's not home from school or wherever he is," Cleveland said. "What can I do for you?"

"I came for my pay," the girl said.

"Pay for what?" Lola said.

"I've been down in your ravine. I raked it and hauled off all the bottles and trash. I got the rest of the fence out. I dug up the posts and rolled the barbed wire and turned the earth over in the side garden back of the garage. And I put down the Vigoro. I did some weeding too, if you want to come look at it." She sounded tired and a little angry.

"I don't get it. I pay a man for my gardening," Cleveland

said. "All this heavy work you're talking about, I pay a man for."

"You pay my father," the girl said. "He has the fever and chills today and couldn't do his work, so I did it."

"You're Jack's daughter?" Cleveland said.

"Stephanie," the girl said, nodding. She took off a thick glove and stuck it over the top of the shovel. She lit a cigarette from a rumpled pack of Chesterfields. "Howdy said start in wherever Dad quit and do what I could, as much as possible."

Cleveland said, "You wait there, sweetheart, for just a second." He motioned for Lola to follow him back away from the door.

Maureen stayed with the gardener's daughter and said, "I wish I could get my hair to curl like yours."

When Maureen and the girl were out of earshot, Cleveland whispered, "Her daddy's a drinker. I bet he's home with a snootful."

"Well, it's him you hired to do the yardwork, not his children," Lola said. "She looks like she's been working, though."

"I know. It's all right for today. Today it was just the heavy work. I'll sign a check for you to fill out for whatever Howdy promised—within reason. But you tell her this is the only time. We don't want to set any precedents. And you tell her that if her father's sick, he should phone *me*."

"And not Howdy, right?" Lola said.

"I'll skin that Howdy when I catch up to him," Cleveland said. "It's all right for today. She couldn't do any damage to the ravine. But I don't want some amateur trying to trim hedges and grow azaleas. That's tricky work and that's what I pay her dad for."

"She's the ugliest thing I've ever seen," Lola said.

"I wouldn't say that," Cleveland said. "But my left shoe is prettier." He headed for the kitchen, calling Virginia.

The MG revved in the driveway as Lola went back to the door. Howdy was gliding up in neutral, tapping the accelerator. When he jumped from the car, Lola saw fresh paint drizzled all over his new jump suit.

"You boss is home," Lola said to the gardener's daughter. The girl looked, cigarette smoke trailing from her nostrils.

"I'm glad you're still here, Steph," Howdy said. He put his arm around her neck. "You're staying for supper." He had smears of paint on the corners of his mouth from holding a brush in his teeth. "Did you meet Daddy? This is my sister Maureen, and this is Lola."

"We met," Lola said.

Howdy was still hugging the girl. He tried to kiss her face but she ducked away. "We went out on a field trip," Howdy said. "We went out to the quarry to paint the rocks."

"That's what we need," Lola said. "More painted rocks."

"Hey, Maureen, this is Stephanie." Howdy squeezed the girl again. "Did Daddy pay you yet?"

"We're thinking about it," Lola said.

"I love her hair," Maureen said.

"I love her hair, too. You're going to eat with us," Howdy said. He put his nose over the girl's ear. She twisted away.

"Eat what?" Lola said.

"I gotta go," Stephanie said.

"The hell you do," Howdy said. "Come on, Steph. Come inside. I want to show you around."

Stephanie flicked her cigarette into the shrubs. "I just want to get paid so I can go," she said.

Howdy put his head on her shoulder. He said, "Oh, Steph, no."

12

The candle flames twitched in the night breeze that moved through the dining-room screens. The long cherry table had been set for four. Between the pewter candelabra was a cut-glass pitcher of whiskey sours with orange slices floating on top. Lola was ladling consommé into little tureens and passing them around.

Cleveland and Virginia sat at either end of the table. Howdy and Maureen were facing each other. Howdy was jabbering. He shook salt into his soup and then onto his salad. "So I saw this miserable-looking girl out in the terrible rain with the campus gardening crew. She and a bunch of campus maintenance guys were feeding branches from a tree into this huge shredder. You should have heard the noise. It was horrible."

"Oh, shut up," Lola said.

"I tell you I saw this petite waif in the rain feeding this fire-breathing dragon of a machine and I was really touched."

"Touched in the head," Cleveland said. He spooned some soup into his mouth. "Lola, this soup tastes too good to be good for me."

"Yes, it is very rich and very good," Virginia said. "Lola is such an angel."

"So, naturally, I went up to this girl and started talking to her," Howdy said.

Lola took a bottle of low-cal salad dressing from the pocket of her smock and smacked the bottle down on the table. "I forgot this," she said.

"It turned out the girl was Stephanie and that her father works for us, so I asked her to a movie," Howdy said.

Maureen's glasses were cocked up on her forehead, pushing back her short bangs. Before her on the table were two empty cans of beer and a half-drained glass of whiskey.

"For Christ's sake, Lola, sit down and eat," Cleveland said. "Take a load off."

"Who'd bring in the food?" Lola said.

Howdy poured himself a fresh drink from the pitcher. "Steph's family lived in an apartment underneath a disturbed woman in Florida. This woman lived upstairs and was always trying to commit suicide."

"The poor thing," Virginia said.

Howdy said, "They knew, because the woman always talked about killing herself."

"Great," Lola said.

"Stephanie said it was really something," Howdy said. He moved his salad around and plunged his fork into the lettuce.

"Why?" Virginia said.

"Lola, will you sit down?" Maureen said.

"I don't get paid to sit down," Lola said.

"Well," Howdy said, munching, "so this woman disappeared for a week one time. She stopped roaming the halls and her morning papers and mail stacked up, but Stephanie's family could hear her up there walking around."

"Well, good," said Virginia.

"No, wait'll you hear," Howdy said, wagging his fork. "So then Steph and her whole family hear the bathtub filling up upstairs. They all listened to it."

"Throw me that salad dressing," Cleveland said.

"*Listen*, Dad," Howdy said. "So Steph's family got worried, hearing the bathwater and all. So they called the landlord, who comes over with a key."

"Really?" Virginia said.

"Yes," Howdy said. "The landlord went into the place and the woman was dead. She'd killed herself. But when the coroner and the police came, they said she'd been dead at least five days."

"Oh, how sad," Virginia said.

"That means Stephanie's a big liar," Maureen said.

"No," Howdy said, "the whole family heard the woman moving around."

"The whole family was drunk," Cleveland said. "I need the pepper."

"Well, believe what you want, but that's what happened. Steph doesn't know how to lie, and as far as booze goes, she doesn't touch it." Howdy had some more of his whiskey. "I'm going to marry Stephanie."

Maureen lit a cigarette and blew a smoke ring at the ceiling. Lola went into the kitchen.

The phones rang. "That's Steph!" Howdy sprang up. "I told her to call me at eight thirty." He took his drink with him and left the room.

Virginia and Maureen were quiet, their eyes on Cleveland, who was finishing his soup. He spanked the bottle of dressing, and decorated his salad. Lola brought in the chicken and sat down in Howdy's chair. She watched Cleveland as he tossed his salad leaves with his fork.

"All right," he said, and put down the fork. He poured from the pitcher into his glass and drank. "Don't look at me."

"He can't marry her," Lola said. "She doesn't even like him."

"This is just some Howdy idea," Cleveland said. "It'll go away like all the others. Goddamn his screwball mother! And you, Maureen."

"Me! What?" Maureen said.

"Yes, you. For setting the example. For having a baby at fifteen. For living off your father."

"*Me*?" Maureen said. "Howdy's four years older than me."

"Shall I powder my nose?" Virginia said.

Lola picked up a cherry tomato from Howdy's salad. She said, "I forgot to eat today."

"My hors d'oeuvres!" Maureen said, and jumped up. She went into the kitchen and used a dish towel to pull out a broiler pan covered over with little sausages wrapped in bacon and stuck with toothpicks. She carried them back to the dining table.

"You do real well," Cleveland said. "You're twenty-four, and without Lola you'd starve."

"These weren't for me," Maureen said. "They're meat. I don't eat meat anymore. They were for you and Virginia, so you could have something hot." She tipped the pan and let the charred sausages roll off and bounce onto the table. Virginia yelped and shoved back in her chair.

"Help yourself," Maureen said.

"Nothing more for her to drink," Cleveland said to Lola. "And don't you dare clean that up. Let her."

Maureen sat down and finished her whiskey. "It's boiling hot in here," she said. "Can't we turn the air conditioner back on?"

Howdy bounded back into the room and pulled a chair over to the table. He lifted one of Maureen's black hors d'oeuvres from where it had landed in the sugar bowl. He juggled it from palm to palm. "Hot," he said. "Who threw these out for us?"

"Maureen did it," Virginia said.

"Thanks," Howdy said. "Steph and I were talking about Europe for a honeymoon. *I* was talking about it, actually. She hasn't said yes yet."

"God bless her," Lola said.

"I haven't been to Europe since the war," Cleveland said. "It was a very untidy continent at the time."

"Which war was this?" Howdy said.

"Think about it," Maureen said to her brother.

"Oh." Howdy bit into the sausage.

"Europe costs a fortune," Cleveland said. "Dan and Elsie Willinger just got back, and Dan told me they paid eight dollars for a sweet roll and a Coke in Paris."

"God," Virginia said.

"Dan Willinger's head of quality control for me," Cleveland said.

"We'd skip Paris," Howdy said. "We'd bike around and backpack and stay in hostels."

"Still," Cleveland said, "there'd be your fares over and back."

Howdy thought a moment. "Well, sure. But we can get jobs and stack up some dough. Steph can do lots of things. I heard about a job I can get reading best-sellers onto tapes for blind people."

"You two could work your way over on a tramp steamer," Maureen said.

"Yeah," Howdy said, "stuff like that."

Cleveland was chewing at a piece of chicken. "And here's a thought," he said. "Why don't you take Lola? You'll need somebody to see to your clothes and get your reservations for you and put some decent meals together at roadside after the long days of bicycling in the Alps and to figure out that foreign money."

"Steph and I want to go alone," Howdy said.

"Oh, hell," Cleveland said, "and here I was getting ready to get a passport and oil my bicycle chain."

"Violet would love to go," Maureen said. "Why not take Violet, Howdy?"

Howdy thumped down his fist and the tableware rattled. "Settle down!" he shouted.

Virginia giggled. "I think there's something on my foot." She ducked her head under the table.

Maureen went to the kitchen and poured soda into one of Violet's Tweetie Pie tumblers. She tonged in some ice from a metal bucket. There was a loud banging on the kitchen door.

She yanked it open and said, "*Now* what?"

Chris cuffed the frame of the door and came inside. He had bathed and shaved. His clean hair reflected light and he smelled of soap. He had changed his clothes. He was dressed in a pale shirt, summery trousers, moccasins.

Maureen turned her back to him and started for the dining

room. Chris followed her. He grabbed her by the arms. "Let go, please," she said. "I don't want to spill Violet's drink."

"Who are you talking to?" Cleveland yelled from the table.

"No one, Daddy! Never mind!" She said, "Chris, for the last time, I'm serious. Leave me alone."

"Why?" he said.

"You know why." She whirled, swatted at him, and missed. Chris laughed, and Maureen said, "I swear to God, you make me insane." She tossed the soda into his face. He spun away, and she pounded him between the shoulder blades with her fist.

Cleveland came to the doorway with Lola behind him just as Chris was turning on Maureen, his open palm raised and ready to slap her.

"Don't do it!" Lola barked.

"My Lord," Cleveland said.

"Bastard," Maureen said.

Chris wiped his face on his sleeve. "I only came to get my shirt—the one Mo was wearing today. That's all I came for, and to kiss Violet good night."

"Just leave," Maureen said.

"That's right," Cleveland said. "Get in your car and blow before we get a restraining order down on you. What the hell's your problem, anyway?"

"Scram," Lola said.

Chris said, "My daughter is living in a madhouse. That bothers me a lot."

"We don't want to hear it," Cleveland said. "As far as I'm concerned, you were never a father to Violet. You gave up your rights long ago. I don't want to hear one more word about it. You never gave Maureen a red cent. If she wanted to, she could've claimed half your lottery money. Did you ever think of that? It's hers, but she's too decent a person to ask for it. We've done our best for Violet and you haven't done spit."

"I'd marry Maureen. She won't marry me," Chris said.

"Good," Lola said.

Howdy stepped in from the dining room. "There's no reason to yell, is there?" he said. "Hey, really, what's the matter out here?"

"We want Chris to leave and he won't," Maureen said.

"He'll go. One way or another," Cleveland said. He moved up close to Chris.

"You'll give yourself a stroke," Chris said.

Cleveland laughed at him. "Oh? Is that what I'll do?"

"I'll walk you out to your car, Chris. Why don't I?" Howdy said. "I want to hear about living in Canada, because I'm getting married soon and my bride and I are thinking about moving to Canada."

"I don't need anybody to walk me to my car," Chris said. He wiped his face again. "I'll come back tomorrow when you're all sober."

"I wouldn't do that," Lola said.

"Just try," Cleveland said. "I'll have you in the pokey for life imprisonment."

"You're all crazy," Chris said.

Maureen said, "Why don't you just drive yourself off a bridge somewhere? Do me and Violet a favor and go erase yourself."

"I'll see to you first," Chris said, his voice trembling.

"I interpret that remark as a threat, boy," Cleveland said. "I'm a witness to one of my children being threatened. You're going to jail for that. You better get out of here because the forces of justice are about to descend on you."

Maureen started crying.

Chris brought a cigarette from his breast pocket. "Does anybody have a light? My matches seem to be wet for some reason."

"I don't believe this," Howdy said, smiling.

"Call the police," Lola said.

"Everyone's lit and no one has matches? What'll you tell

the police?" Chris said, his cigarette waggling between his lips. "They'll lock the bunch of you up."

"Will you just quit this?" Maureen sobbed.

Chris wheeled around and ambled out the kitchen door.

Maureen went to the windows in the breakfast room. She stood watching as Chris walked along the driveway. He stopped at Virginia's car. He used the cigarette lighter on the dashboard. Maureen dried her eyes with her fists. She went back to the counter and poured another glass of soda pop for Violet.

Cleveland sighed and threw his big arm around her. Lola bustled back and forth. She dished a pudding dessert into stemmed cups. She sprinkled cinnamon on top.

The front-door chimes sounded again. Maureen's lips tightened. She grabbed up the glass of soda and headed through the dining hall to the foyer. Howdy cringed a little. He said, "Couldn't we let Lola answer that?"

"No!" Maureen screamed. She flung open the door. A township policeman was standing on the porch, holding Violet's hand.

"Does this belong here?" the policeman said. He had a new-looking mustache.

"Of course," Maureen said. "Why? Where was she? Violet, where were you?"

"She's all right, Miss," the policeman said. "Try to calm down."

"What?" Maureen said.

"I just went out," Violet said. "I'm all right."

"Out to where?" Maureen said.

"The lights from my cruiser picked her up," the policeman said. "She was jumping around near the road. Dressed like this."

"Well, it's not exactly cold," Maureen said.

"It's dark," the policeman said.

"Violet, why did you go out?" Maureen said. "Tell me, and it better be good. I really could throttle you. Not really," she mouthed to the officer.

"I just went for a minute," Violet said.

The policeman said, "You might tell her, Miss, that we've got some bad characters running loose. Ones that might startle a little girl or even do worse. I've seen a lot of bad characters."

"I'll tell her," Maureen said. She pulled Violet to her.

"Good night, now," the policeman said. "You stay in your nice house, little girl."

"I promise," Violet said.

"Thank you," Maureen called as the policeman turned away. He sauntered, hips jiggling, down to the turnaround, where his cruiser was parked, its red beacon beating.

Howdy sidled into the foyer. "Violet, I'm happy to see you up," he said. "Uncle Howdy's getting married!"

Maureen said, "You're lucky, Violet. You realize you're a very lucky girl? He might have thrown us all in prison. Now take this son-of-a-bitch soda."

"Wish me best wishes," Howdy said. "Congratulate your uncle, the groom."

13

I could guiltlessly murder you," Maureen said. She waved Violet's top sheet in the air, then let it float down over the small body.

"I have two things," Violet said, holding up two fingers.

Maureen stuffed the sheet under the mattress as she moved around the canopied bed. "They'd better be short and sweet."

"Okay," Violet said. "Number one is this finger. Number two is the other one."

Maureen tucked the sheet under Violet's chin, which Violet had made fat by tilting down her face.

Violet pulled her arms and shoulders out from under. "Can I ask you a favor?"

Maureen sighed, looked at the ceiling, put her hands on her hips. "What?"

"Can we camp out on the den floor tonight and have a slumber party?"

"I'd do it, Violet, but Grandpa hates it so much in the morning. He hates to see us asleep, period. Besides, you've been too bad."

"Please, please," Violet said. "Come on, Mom."

"Okay, here's what I'll do," Maureen said. "I'll go to the bathroom and take a bath, and if you're asleep when I come back, I'll think about it and probably we can do it."

"Can Howdy do it, too?"

"I'll ask him, but only if you're really, truly asleep when I'm finished with my bath."

14

The water made the house pipes thunder. Maureen lined up her bath things on the outside ledge of the tub. She undressed and put on a long yellow robe. She went for an ashtray.

At the end of the hall there was TV light from the den. She found Howdy sitting on the back of the sofa. He was feeding himself from a bag of potato chips.

"Come and watch Jack Benny," he said.

Maureen plopped down by his feet. "I can't now. I'm taking a bath."

"Benny's going to Palm Springs," Howdy said. "It's that one. We've seen it."

"Get me a beer," Maureen said.

Howdy went obediently to the kitchen. Maureen crossed her legs and sat back. She had been slogging various drinks most of the day, and had the beginnings of a drunk going.

In the front windows, the sky sputtered pink with heat lightning.

"Why do you like people, Howdy?" Maureen said, taking the beer bottle from him.

"You mean the human race?"

"You once said it was my big problem," Maureen said.

Howdy climbed up onto the back of the sofa again, and went to work on the potato chips.

"I hate life," Maureen said.

"Go hate it in the garage," he said. "Let me see Jack Benny."

"It's not me I feel sorry for. It's Violet—what I've done to her. It's too late for her. The handwriting's on the wall and I can see it in her eyes. She's going to be miserable as soon as whatever chemicals that protect children wear off. Sometimes I think she'd be better off dead."

Howdy munched and crossed his legs. "I'm not saying that's a sick way of thinking," he said. "Because I'm surprised every day we don't all kill each other. But I think you, specifically, expect too much, Mo. All young people do, but you really expect the most of anybody I've ever heard of. Don't you think it's great that we try so hard to be good and do the right thing? And, okay, it's predictable that we fail, but so what? Did I ever show you those photographs I have that were taken by a German woman right after World War Two? Oh, God, if I didn't, I should go get them right now. They're so beautiful. Of reunions. Hungry, grateful faces."

"My bath's going to run over. Anyway, I hate World War Two, and I never ever want to think about it," Maureen said.

She hurried back through the hall. She threw off her robe and put herself into the water. She lay on her spine, knees bent, and let beer spill down both corners of her mouth as she swigged from the bottle. Her free hand paddled the water, working up suds from the soap powder that had settled on the bottom.

Through the door, Howdy said, in a loud whisper: "One

more thing. If Violet acts happy it's not on account of some kid chemical. There are lots of morose kids, and even lots who kill themselves, and you can't say they're protected by being so young. If Violet were wretchedly miserable, and you'd ruined her, that's exactly how she'd act."

Maureen said, "Thank you. Howdy? Do you want to sleep in the house tonight? I mean, instead of at your place? Violet wants me to have a slumber party with her."

"Please can we, Howdy?" Maureen heard Violet from somewhere outside the door.

"Violet! Are you up? What did I tell you! You tell me what I said about getting up!"

"Settle down," Howdy said. "Listen, I'll throw some stuff together and we'll watch the Charlie Chan movie that's coming on. Dad won't like it, but what do we care?"

"Yeah, what do we care about Dad?" Maureen said, and slid back down into the bubbly water.

Two

1

Violet ate sleepily from Howdy's bag of potato chips. She was on the sofa, almost obscured by the heavy bolster pillow on her lap. Rain was drizzling noiselessly onto the lawn, but the night had cooled only a little since dinner. Howdy had worked hard on their floor bed. He was still shaking and smoothing down the layers and layers of sheets and blankets. "This is a bed," he said.

Maureen said, "I'll say. Are you happy now, Violet?"

"Yes," Violet said.

Maureen went to the dark kitchen. Deep in the big refrigerator she found the last carton of Rolling Rock, and a note from Lola: "He who pops the first cap on these must restock the entire supply." Maureen took half the bottles and carried them against her chest back to the den. On the TV screen the opening credits for *Charlie Chan in Honolulu* were rolling.

"Do we have to see this movie?" Violet said.

"We have to see it," Howdy said.

"It's all that's on," Maureen said. "Would you rather sleep in your room?"

"I think so." Violet dragged herself from the sofa and shambled toward the hallway.

"You're kidding," Howdy said.

"Just let her go," Maureen said.

Howdy got off his knees and slung a sofa cushion at the floor. "Violet, you little traitor!"

"Good night, kiddo," Maureen called to her daughter. "And scrub your teeth after eating that junk. God, you'd think we were hillbillies who never heard of nutrition."

"Good night," the little voice answered.

"Only a mother could overlook this," Howdy said. "What total ingratitude." He stared at his slumber-party creation and then at Maureen.

"Go ahead. You can have it," she said.

"Naw, I'd feel stupid."

"Yeah, you'll feel stupid but do it anyway."

"I'd feel stupid when Lola finds me."

"This looks good. Let's watch it awhile," Maureen said. "We can decide later where we're going to sleep."

Two-thirds of the way through *Charlie Chan in Honolulu,* Cleveland came home. His hair was damp and there was mist on his shoes. When he said hello, he looked at the furniture and not at his children. He spent time in the kitchen and then brought in a bowl of Lola's soup and four pieces of cold chicken. "Haven't you all seen every one of these by now?" He waved a piece of chicken at the TV.

Howdy said, "We half-watched this one once, but we missed a lot. There was company here, or something."

"I know I've seen this one," Cleveland said. "The ship's captain is the culprit. He did it."

"That's good," Howdy said.

Cleveland slurped his soup. When he was through eating, he drank from a plastic bottle of antacid. "Fire down below," he said. He pressed his hand on his belly.

"How was your evening?" Maureen said.

Cleveland shifted his position a little. He took another swallow of antacid. "I don't know," Cleveland said.

"I'm trying to concentrate," Howdy said.

Cleveland said, "So after we didn't go to Bacon's, we didn't go to La Scala."

"I remember that place," Maureen said. "We went there for my—something. Not graduation."

"You didn't have a graduation," Cleveland said. "It must have been for the something."

"I know, Dad," Maureen said.

"It was for Chris's winning the lottery," Cleveland said. "Anyway. Where we did go was to Virginia's condominium."

"Yeah?" Maureen said.

"So that's where we went, and since you're both supposed to be adults, that's what we did."

"Oo la la," Howdy said. "Virginia, I must say!"

Maureen waited a couple of beats, and said, "That's the most pathetic, most irresponsible thing I've ever heard of. How could you behave like that, and what an asinine idea for you to tell me and Howdy. You didn't tell us because we're adults. You told us because you wanted to brag. It was completely wrong for you to tell us. Jesus God," Maureen said. "It was wrong for you to tell us because Howdy and I know this whole romance is a fake. You don't love this Virginia person and she certainly doesn't love you. She was pie-eyed from the whiskey sours probably. Or she was lonely, and deservedly so. It's bad enough when people have indiscriminate sex, but at your age it's disgusting. You don't care for that absurd woman. Can you tell us you care about her one iota?"

"Maureen," Howdy said, uneasily.

"Let her talk," Cleveland said.

"You're pitiful," Maureen said.

Howdy got down on his floor bed. He stared at the television screen.

Cleveland stood with aching slowness and stacked his plate and bowl on the shelf behind the couch.

Maureen stared at her bandaged toe.

"All right," Cleveland said, and then he walked out of the room.

Howdy and Maureen watched the Charlie Chan movie until it switched to a new one called *Home Before Dark*.

"Oh, this is good," Maureen said, tearing at her thumbnail with her teeth.

Howdy stood up and straightened the legs of his jump suit.

"Man, oh, man," he said before he left for his place.

2

Charity Way was the country club's road. It started at the club's swimming pool, ran along and eventually bisected the golf course. A mile in, at the head of the Cleveland drive, were evergreen shrubs and a stand of birch trees. The lazy driveway ran off at a right angle to the face of the Cleveland house—a masonry and stone affair, a sort of rambling chateau with a slate roof and chimney pots. At a bent elbow in the drive was a copse of planting that surrounded an Italian bronze nymph. The girl stood in perpetual surprise, improbably balanced on the ball of a slender foot. Her lips were parted and her large eyes were rolled back to look forever over her shoulder.

The drive split; the left fork ended in a shallow court in front of the new garage. The right meandered through straight poplars, then turned back on itself past the old garage and servants' quarters. Above was Howdy's place. The front was an array of louvered doors that gave onto a balcony with a tulip garden. Inside was a fully equipped kitchen and dining annex, hardwood floors scattered with Indian rugs and rush mats, walls painted a light stone color. The living area had a new striped sofa. A junk sculpture of Howdy's hung on the north wall, auto parts welded into a roughly square shape. Also on the wall were several enormous canvases, all bad, all signed "Sarah, 78." The room had redwood shelving where a library of theater-related books was braced: plays, criticism, drama reviews. In a corner stood a plaster woman wearing a black corset and garters. There were nine or ten plants set about in pots and baskets.

Stephanie lay naked on her stomach on Howdy's bed under a clean flannel sheet. The floor-length pleated curtains were drawn open beside her, and the little paved area behind the garage was shadowy and blue in the patchy moonlight.

Howdy strolled into the bedroom and then went out again to put on a record, Mahler. Stephanie sat up and pulled at her frazzled hair, getting it to crowd her skinny face. Howdy came back, braying along with the record and toting two glasses of brandy. His drinking glasses, like Violet's, had cartoon characters etched on their sides—Yosemite Sam and Daffy Duck.

"I didn't mean for you to wait up, Steph, after you worked so hard. Good God in heaven, I'm nervous about the play. Do you realize it's the night after tomorrow? No, wait, that can't be. Yes! It's the night after tomorrow."

"I slept since five o'clock," Stephanie said. She yawned mightily, raising her arms in the air, watching Howdy as he watched her.

He put one of the glasses between her meager breasts. "You're just like a boy when you yawn."

"I done myself, twice, waiting for you," she said. "I was bored, I guess." She wrinkled her puffy eyes at him.

"I'm glad, honey, because I'm all in tonight. Man, you should've heard my sister. She went nuts. She practically destroyed my dad."

Stephanie took the glass and sniffed it and handed it back. "No, thank you," she said.

Howdy drank both brandies quickly, then got out of his jump suit and shoes and under the sheet with her.

"Am I working tomorrow?"

"Hell, no," Howdy said. "I can't have my fiancée mowing the lawn! Pretty soon, my family'll even be able to know you're staying here some nights. I'm old enough, and it's time Dad knew it."

"I need the money," Stephanie said.

"Don't worry about money. Worry about my play."

"Worry about this," she said, reaching between his legs.

"No dice," he said. "What I really want to do is go in the living room and go over my script awhile. You can cue me."

3

The main house had been built in the twenties by a newspaper publisher. Lola's bedroom was on the first floor just to the west of the elaborate blue brass-fitted front doors.

Lola sat on her bed and pulled a white wool sock on over her foot. It was still dark, though nearly dawn. A soft gust of rain whispered on her window screens.

"Rumors," she said. She went to her bureau and, without checking in the round mirror on the stand there, fitted a shell comb in her hair. She hefted a school text, *Personnel: Standard Management Techniques*. She took the book with her out through the foyer and into the family den. There were low gunshots and a smattering of yelps from the television. Maureen was lying awake in the complicated arrangement of sheets and blankets, her chin propped on a fringed pillow.

She sat up to hunt for a cigarette. "I haven't slept all night, I swear."

Lola paid no attention. "I've got to concentrate on the books, but no one here will let me alone. The school said if they let me back in I'd have to do well. Being on academic probation means you do well or forget about it. It's expected you don't just do average. But who cares? Do you care, with your messiness? Dropping things, always dropping things the minute you're done with them."

"Where's your other sock?" Maureen said, blinking. With her pointed knuckle she shut down the television.

Lola moved toward the kitchen. "Violet?" she yelled. "Violet, you come in here right now!"

Maureen curled her toes and arched her back in a yawn that popped some bones.

"Violet!" Lola yelled.

From the end of the long central corridor, far back in the house, Violet said, "What's wrong? What did I do?"

Lola came back into the den long enough to turn on the overhead light and scream for Violet. The child came, stumbling, open-mouthed, her eyes slivers. Maureen reached her arm out and Violet fell down beside her. "This is funny," Maureen said. "Lola's walking and talking in her sleep."

"Why did she want me?" Violet said.

"She doesn't know what she wants," Maureen said. "But I don't think we're supposed to wake her up."

"She's not asleep."

"Yeah, she is," Maureen said.

"Poor Violet," Lola said. She had the schoolbook under one arm and a casserole pan in her hand. "My father's going to whip you."

"Who's her father?" Violet said, holding onto Maureen. "The one that ate the peppers?"

"Pay no attention. She's probably dreaming something, and you just happened to fit in," Maureen said.

Lola began addressing an empty armchair. "Don't drive so fast. What did you get me for Christmas?" Lola said to the chair.

"Zombie!" Violet whispered.

"Poor child. Poor everybody," Lola said. She turned around and went back through the foyer to her bedroom. Violet followed on her tiptoes. From the doorway, she watched as Lola crawled carefully back under the covers with the book and the pan still in her hands.

4

Violet rotated the channel selector, clicking past varieties of electronic snow. She spun back to a station with two men insulting one another.

"Lie still now and turn that way down," Maureen said. With Violet beside her, she focused on one of the front windows. Out in the yard, a dogwood tree was materializing from the ground mist. One of the men on the TV show was saying, "Our primary concern is not matching funds, but the interdependent children. What the mayor does with the budget interests us as citizens, but not as administrators of a relief project."

"You call it a relief project?" the other man said.

Maureen went in and out of sleep until a phrase of violin music caused her to open her eyes. The den was full of sun. On the TV a Japanese girl in a business suit was playing Bach. Her pretty, flat face was tipped sideways over her instrument. A hank of black hair glinted on her cheekbone. "Go back where you came from," Maureen said.

She looked around, and saw that Violet was gone.

She slid open the glass door in the back wall of the den. On the brick veranda sat her father in a wrought-iron chair at a wrought-iron table. He was in a splash of light that came through the roof of spaced wooden beams and was strained through the webs of ivy. He wore work clothes, his faded chinos and a rumpled blue shirt. He poured from a pitcher of orange juice and wiped his hand dry on his trousers.

"My God, I'm sorry," Maureen said. She took a seat on the bricks. "I honestly swear I didn't mean what I said, whatever I said."

"I'm not made of glass," Cleveland said. "A kid like you can't even chip me with a hammer."

"I'm really sorry," Maureen said.

Cleveland sipped his orange juice. He watched her carefully. "Ginny's coming for lunch," he said.

"Good, good. I want to make up with her. I feel guilty about her too."

"She's not your business," Cleveland said.

"I know that. I really do," Maureen said. "Hey, where's Vi?"

Cleveland folded an arm across his chest and scratched the outside of his elbow. "Down in her play yard, I think. Lola gave her breakfast."

"Already? What time is it?"

"Going on ten," Cleveland said.

"That's hard to believe," Maureen said.

"Don't believe it!" Howdy came in yelling. "It's really ten after nine. Daddy, you always lie and make it an hour ahead of time." He joined them on the veranda. He had a cereal bowl of creamed oatmeal and a mug of tea. He looked tousled and pale in his spattered jump suit. He hadn't shaved yet or combed his hair. "He's just trying to make you feel lazy and guilty, Mo."

"She *is* lazy and guilty," Cleveland said.

"You just do that time stuff to make everybody feel bad. You always used to do it to Mom." Howdy spooned up his cereal, pausing only to stomp a wasp that, wounded mortally, stayed stuck to his shoe. When his oatmeal was gone, he swallowed his tea, and filled up the mug with orange juice.

"You don't want any of that," Cleveland said. "I accidentally spilled gasoline in it."

Howdy passed the cup under his nose. "Screwdrivers! No wonder you look so happy."

"Remember your stomach, Dad," Maureen said.

"Drinking before noon. You know what that means?" Howdy said. "First sign of dipsomania. That's what it means."

"I'm scared to death," Cleveland said.

5

Maureen followed Violet's trail past the toolshed and through a thicket of young birches that screened the back side of the house from the road. Violet's yard was a sodded peninsula of land between the deepest part of the ravine and Charity Way. She had swings there, pipe scaffolding for climbing, a rusted merry-go-round horse on a massive coil of spring. Violet was in the horse's saddle, holding on to the hemp reins and rocking wildly. Behind her was a dilapidated badminton net and, out of the shade on ruined grass, an empty inflatable pool.

Maureen's bare feet brushed the wet lawn. The sun, already hot, was picking out each blade of grass, every sprig of weed and clover. An S-shape—a muddy black slash—moved by her foot. She saw an eye with a tiny sun reflected in its dead center. She screamed.

"You okay, Mom?" Violet said.

Maureen sprinted for the jungle gym and clambered aboard. "I saw a snake."

"Howdy says they won't hurt you. Was it black?"

"Yeah, I know it won't hurt me," Maureen said. From far

down the ravine, she heard the beating noise of a helicopter.

On the other side of the little chasm, across the road, someone cut a golf club, socked a ball, yelled, "Oh, Christ, I don't believe it!"

Violet rocked the horse, driving its nose so far forward it nearly touched the ground, then she yanked back so that she faced the sky.

"You'll break your spine," Maureen said.

"Watch!" Violet said, and on a forward thrust she pushed out of the iron stirrups and scrambled in the air—a floppy doll in a checkered playsuit. She landed heavily on her side.

Maureen dropped over the top rail of the jungle gym, hurrying to extract herself from the maze of pipes. But Violet was instantly on her feet and running for the swings.

6

As the day wore on, Maureen and Violet strapped on bikini bathing suits and spent almost an hour blowing up Violet's swimming pool. They screwed a garden hose to a spigot in the laundry room, and together they wove the length of hose through shrubs and around patio furniture and got the nozzle to reach the pool.

Violet was supine in the few inches of cool water. Maureen lay with her head propped on a softened volleyball. "This is most pleasant," Maureen said.

It was airless where they were, the heat popping and ticking chaotically with bugs.

"Last night, that was so weird," Violet said.

"You mean Lola?"

"Can I be the one that tells her?" Violet said.

"Sure. I don't care," Maureen said.

"I know where she is. I saw her in that red scarf at the window of Grandma's—I mean, Grandpa's—piano room."

"Cripes, you're afraid to say *Grandma*?"

"I am not."

"You are too. I can tell."

They were quiet a while. Violet drifted her fingers to and fro in the water.

"I'm not mad at you," Maureen said at last. "Of course, you're terrified to use the name Grandma around here. *I* practically am. But that piano was strictly your grandma's property. Can you think of anyone else who plays? Not counting Uncle Howdy because that's not playing. I wish I had a recording of your grandmother. She could sing so splendidly. Now spit that out, Violet. Gad!"

Violet had been sitting up paddling the water with a plastic Frisbee. She had let the Frisbee fill and drunk from it. She was staring back at her mother, her cheeks ballooned.

"Spit it out!" Maureen said.

Violet swallowed.

"Ooh, yeck, Violet. Why would you do that? Don't you know people's feet have been in this water?" Maureen snatched the Frisbee and sent it out into the grass under the swings.

"Mine are clean," Violet said, showing her feet, the skin puckered and fish-belly white.

"Yeah, where do you think the dirt went?" Maureen said.

Violet got out of the pool, flexed her knees, squeezed her hair into wet pigtails, creased her nose at the sun, and marched haughtily in place a dozen beats. Then she threw herself onto the ground on her stomach. "Tell me what else about Grandma?"

"I will in a second," Maureen said. "First I want to finish with this other, immediate thing. Never ever do that again. There are countless diseases in this water. They're lying in wait—invisible to us—in germs." She got cross-legged on the ground before Violet, who was smiling drunkenly from tickling her nostrils with a weed.

"So, as I said, Mother's singing was the thing I really remember. She did it in a startlingly high voice called a soprano. Mine is like below that. A contralto, or whatever. And the whole time she worked around the house, she sang, too. If you heard her, you knew she was cleaning."

"Wouldn't Lola clean?" Violet said.

"No, we didn't have Lola then. My father wouldn't hire a maid or cook. Though, if the truth were known, we were even richer than we are now. My mother did every scrap of cleaning herself—*and* the marketing, the meals, the housekeeping, the laundry. Ironed the shirts. See, you don't know this, but your grandpa was a real hick. Only he happened to make a lot of money out of luck or something, but mainly from his soda-pop business. Mother, on the other hand, was loaded with dough to start with. Her parents had each left her buckets of it when they died. Anyway, so she was just raised a different way than your grandpa was. She never expected to have to scrub out the oven or load stuff for the dump. You employed somebody for that if you were like people from Mother's family. They were very mild, very gentle people. Like my mom had this tremor—which means her hands shook, just ever so perceptibly—when she poured tea."

"Aww, Grandma," Violet said.

Maureen was holding out both hands, making them tremble. "You just want to go, don't you?"

"Yeah, but you can still tell me about Grandma after we get Lola."

"No, it's okay. Forget it," Maureen said. "I can't expect you to be interested in someone you've only heard horrifying lies about. But that's what they are, baby—lies. You just remember when your grandpa talks about your grandma, that no matter what he's saying, he's making it all up. Everything about drinking or about ranting and raving? That's all rubbish. If anyone ever drank too much, it was your grandpa. You'll see when we go up to the house. He'll be passed out like a big hog, and it's all from drinking all the time."

7

Lola replaced the light bulb in the emerald-glass lamp in the piano room. She ran her feather duster over the window-sills and on the curly maple frame of an enormous mirror. She put fresh pink marble ashtrays with felt underliners on the stands at either end of the settee. She rested finally on the piano bench before the mirror and watched herself and scratched at a spider bite near her nose. She said to the mirror, " 'The river's face is stuck with a stiff, hard mitten. A blood-stained trace to point out the place, for under the ice lies a dead corpse.' "

"You're putting me on," Cleveland said, his head in the doorway.

Lola stayed in the mirror, with Cleveland's reflection beside her, only smaller. "See how you think this sounds." She inhaled and began again.

"I heard it once," Cleveland said. "And I don't need to know the second stanza because that's probably got grappling hooks in it. This is about the Wilshire kid, right? Who went in the pond after his spaniel?"

"I changed it to a river to be on the safe side," Lola said. "There's more room for the kid to drown in, fewer chances of anybody rescuing him."

"That's screwy," Cleveland said. "You can't improve on the circumstances of a kid's death."

"Death's not the topic," Lola said. She drew back her shoulders and lifted her high bust higher. "In the real day-to-day, death seldom happens. Water's the theme. You look caked with dirt," Lola said.

"I've been digging," Cleveland said. "I just wanted to remind you, Ginny's on the way."

"She's coming?"

"Yep," Cleveland said.

"That's still the plan, huh?" Maureen said, flapping through the doors at the other end of the room, Violet with her, walking bent over in imitation of an ape.

"Lola, we have to tell you something," Violet said.

"Fire away," Lola said.

Cleveland said, "Notice the wet feet on both of them."

"Exactly why is Virginia coming over?" Maureen said.

"She'd like to look at a room," Cleveland said. "This room probably."

"What for?" Maureen said.

Violet talked upward to Lola, who was still gazing at the mirror. "You were doing something hilarious. You don't remember?"

"Me hilarious?" Lola said.

"Ginny would like to have her wedding in this room," Cleveland said. "If we ever get married. She's attracted to the colors in here."

"What was I doing?" Lola said. "Was it something bad?"

Maureen said, "You were walking and talking in your sleep."

"You really were," Violet said. "You went, 'What'd you get me for Christmas?' "

"So you're seriously getting married," Maureen said. "And you don't care if your bride sees you blind drunk?"

8

A red sign was bolted to the chain fence at the end of the airport's long glide path. The sign warned motorists about approaching aircraft. There was, however, a gravel apron off the highway, deep and wide enough for five or six cars, and to there Chris had driven and parked.

Oh!

From head on, the jet he chose to watch was a small horizontal bar in the sky over the flat tops of trees. The jet was gauzed over by distance and uncertain in the waves of heat from the highway. Before there was noise, there were the hanging engines, the black windshield, a pinkish flash of color on the undercarriage. The jet seemed to swell and at last a tearing sound split the air over the soybean fields beyond the end of the runway. The jet came faster and as it passed over the trees a quarter-mile out, its relative size became apparent. Its shadow swallowed row after row of bean plants. The roar dragged somewhere behind. The wheels extended like talons. The wings bristled. The jet closed in, nose up, coasting forward, coming lower, and then the roar began to catch up and shake the local earth.

On the roof of his car, Chris ducked, but kept his eyes on the tremendous belly of the machine that covered the sky over him. He spun on his seat, hands mashed against his ears, scooted forward, dropped his heels down against the windshield, and watched the screaming plane shriek to the ground.

He got into his car. With the tape deck too loud, he drove around treeless, dizzying neighborhoods of new houses. He parked in the lot of a Dairy Delight that stood adjacent to the community's hectic acre of swimming pool. He bought and sucked a slush drink. He sat in his car, looking at the girls in bathing suits, admiring a particular girl in a wet white onepiece that she had outgrown the year before. He exhaled at her through locked teeth. The girl in white stood with her weight on one foot, her breasts pointing.

He took his car downtown and left it on the roof of a public parking garage. On the front lawn of the art gallery, a string quintet sawed away. People lounged or stood in groups on the grass and ate lunches from boxes as they listened to the music.

He walked around to the new wing of the gallery. He breathed the cooled air inside and rode a chromed escalator to the top floor, where a patio gave a view of a cascading, terraced interior garden.

An old man in a uniform, hair growing to his shoulders, walked over to the railing where Chris leaned. "Is it raining?" the man asked.

"It's dry where I've been," Chris said.

"Put out that cigarette," the old man said.

Chris sat on a pew of blond wood and studied a huge sheet-metal sculpture that resembled a lobster. He got up and left. He fetched his car. He drove to the university, parked in a faculty slot in the central quad. He went to the basement of Digby Hall, a brick affair with a gambrel roof and dormer windows. In the basement there was a tiny auditorium and two L-shaped classrooms. This was the school's Drama Department.

Chris went along a narrow passageway that led to the department's green room. He made instant coffee from a kicked-in kettle on a hot plate.

A young woman with a face like an antelope's marched in and stirred up a cup of tea. She wore a man's pajama top, complicated earrings, a miniskirt, short boots.

"Is Howdy Cleveland somewhere around here?" Chris said.

"Are you his lover?" the woman whispered, smiling.

"No, are you?" Chris said.

The woman snorted through slender nostrils.

"I'll start again," Chris said.

"Would you like to have me?" the woman said.

"Have you what?" Chris said.

"Would you like to do me?" the woman said. "You'd be the first, I swear." She unbuttoned her pajama top and opened it. "You're so gorgeous," she said.

Chris went back out into the hall and stopped a fellow with a big black beard. "Do you know Howdy Cleveland?" Chris said.

"I won't say I do and I won't say I don't," the young man said.

The hallway was filling with students. Chris threaded a path through them, asking for Howdy. A boy in blue said, "Check the lunch bar. He likes the lunch bar."

Chris climbed some old stairs and hurried out along a covered walkway that led to the school's cafeteria. He saw Howdy in a circular booth, his nose bent over a tray of sandwiches and waxed paper cups of beer. A skinny girl with a bad complexion and a nest of frizzled hair was at his elbow. A man and woman, both in white T-shirts, both smoking cigarettes, were in the booth as well.

Chris said, "Hey, Howdy."

Howdy pushed his fingers through his hair, making it stand straight up. "What are you doing here, Chris?"

"I was going to eat here. I'm scouting the campus for an apartment."

"These are Richard and Judy Allen and this is Stephanie," Howdy said. He hugged the small girl next to him. "My fiancée."

Chris nodded. The woman in the T-shirt blew a plume of smoke into the silence Chris had brought. When she spoke she sounded as if she had sinus trouble. "We are talking about bathrooms and toilet humor." She made her eyes, which were ringed with dark makeup, very wide. Her husband picked up a sandwich. "You're a man," the woman said to Chris. "How would you characterize the graffiti in a men's room?"

"I wouldn't," Chris said.

"Try," the woman said.

"I really don't know," Chris said.

The woman said, "Wouldn't you say it's normally of three types: scatology, sports stuff, and overbidding for anonymous sex of some stripe or other?"

"You already told us that once," Stephanie interrupted.

"Chris wasn't here then," Howdy whispered to her.

The woman ignored them. "Whereas if you ever went into a ladies' room, you'd be very surprised."

"So would the ladies," Chris said.

"Shut up, dear, and listen," the woman said. "You'd be very surprised to find an enormous degree of human compassion and communication in the things that are written on the walls."

The man had taken his sandwich apart on an open napkin. He chewed on a lettuce leaf and, looking straight ahead, muttered something.

"What say?" the woman said coldly.

"It's their dearth of humor," the man said.

"How do you mean?" Stephanie said.

Chris went for a bowl of chili and crackers. He bought a couple of draft beers at a table that held aluminum kegs and tall cups. He drank off one cup immediately while still standing by the table.

Back at the booth, Howdy was talking. The woman was smoking seriously and listening to Howdy. The man and Stephanie were paying no attention.

"Say, Howdy," Chris said, cutting into the discourse.

"Yes?" Howdy said.

"I need a friend out at your house."

"What for?" Stephanie said.

Chris pinched his packet of saltines and then bit off the cellophane. "Who are you?" he asked her.

"A woman," the woman in the T-shirt said.

"She's my fiancée," Howdy said. "I told you."

Stephanie said, "I saw a funny thing in a bathroom once."

"That's good," the man said. He had torn his sandwich to pieces and thrown some of the pieces on the floor. He rolled a corner of sliced ham into a cone.

"You don't have any friends at Dad's right now," Howdy said.

"You think that's fair? I mean, seriously, Howdy, is it?" Chris said. "What did I do?"

"What did you do?" Howdy said.

"Nothing," Chris said. "I've done nothing. Your sister is just so goddamned spooked all the time, she imagines I've done something wrong. She assumes it." He shook his cracker crumbs into his bowl and ate.

"I think Maureen's cute," Stephanie said.

The woman was using the tip of her cigarette to burn holes in the man's disassembled lunch.

"Hey, I'm eating," Chris said.

9

Howdy took Chris and Stephanie to his studio, which was in a corner of the drawing laboratory on the second floor of the Fine Arts Building. The studio was large and had a skylight and a concrete floor and whitewashed walls. From a giant rack made of two-by-fours, Howdy tugged out canvases.

"These are my latest oils," he said. He leaned a picture against his knees. A heavy umber outline had been scratchily drawn around a frank depiction of a nude girl. Within the figure's borders, patches of pink paint served for shading. Resting on the polelike neck was an accurate likeness of Stephanie.

"Isn't he awful?" Stephanie said.

"Do you think so?" Chris said. "I think it's pretty well rendered."

"I mean, to show me naked."

"I tell her over and over it doesn't matter. This is art," Howdy said.

"Besides, it's not me anyhow," Stephanie said. "Not really."

Chris sat on a sawhorse. "Then it's your twin."

"The body is our life model," Howdy explained. "I paint in the body part at life-drawing class, and then I put Steph's head on at home."

"That's pretty sharp," Chris said.

"Which you can tell if you study the body closely," Howdy said. "Steph's is not so voluptuous and saggy."

"I ain't got boobs that big," Stephanie said.

"Let me see the other pictures," Chris said.

Howdy got out more oil paintings, all pink nudes. Chris walked around them. "Here's a side of you I haven't seen, Steph," Chris said.

"That *is* my ass. Can you tell? How could you tell? That one I posed for."

Howdy groaned, straining on his toes to slide a canvas the size of a small wall from an upper slot of the deep wooden racks. One end of the painting dropped. Chris picked up the end, and Howdy moved the picture out, walking backward. His feet tangled and he fell on his rear.

Chris went to the far side of the room and had a cigarette. Howdy and Stephanie struggled a while, turning the painting to get it right.

"My masterwork. My farewell to the plastic arts," Howdy said.

Chris made a low whistle at the canvas, which showed life-sized portraits of Cleveland, Maureen, Violet, Lola, and—Chris guessed—Howdy's mother. The figures stood in a row, hands joined, like a chain of paper dolls. Real clothing had been glued to the surface of the canvas. Chris recognized the tattersall shirt on Maureen's figure. The faces had been varnished with many overlays of color and had the tactile shine of real flesh. Their eyes glistened where bits of glass had been pushed into the paint.

"You see his mom?" Stephanie said.

Howdy had used fluorescent green to represent a nimbus of light around his mother. Her face was white as a mime's, her lips black. An orange Halloween wig had been pasted on for her hair.

"It's far from finished," Howdy said.

"I've got to tell you, Howdy, this is an eerie thing you've done," Chris said. "This is an odd, voodoo thing."

"Thank you," Howdy said.

"You can tell he likes the people," Stephanie said.

"I know," Chris said. "You can see he loves them."

"Thank you," Howdy said. "And wait'll I put Steph in."

10

The main quadrangle was a large lawn with plenty of shade. The brick walkways that divided the quadrangle converged on a round wooden kiosk pasted over with activity announcements. One of them bore a woodcut with the date, time, and place of Howdy's play.

Chris and Howdy and Stephanie were on the grass not far from the kiosk. Stephanie lay on her front, her thin legs kicking idly up in the air. Howdy had run down the zipper of his jump suit and bared his chest and some of his stomach.

Chris walked an oval around them. "I'm frustrated and I'm mad," he said. "And I have a lot of longing bothering me. You have feelings about Steph. I don't want to embarrass you, Howdy, but my feelings are the way yours are, only sort of desperate. And everything's complicated by Violet. I'd like to be able to see her for six minutes without someone showing me the door."

"Well, it's none of my business, but I think you're being too persistent," Howdy said.

"Don't say that," Chris said.

"You should stay away a week or so and let Maureen settle down."

"Hell, I've *been* away," Chris said. "I've been out of her life for nearly two years." He dropped onto his knees and put a hand on Howdy's shoulder. He squeezed the shoulder as he talked. "Maureen wants to see me and have me around. I'm sure of it, Howdy. I'm positive."

"For example, right now," Howdy said, wincing. "How can I listen to you when you're breaking my clavicle?"

Chris straightened his knees, walked off, and then came back. "Do me a favor and talk to them? Just sit them down and say, 'Maureen, Chris is outside. He just wants to chat with you for half an hour. He has important things to say and it would be to everyone's benefit if you listened. When he's done, if you want him to go away forever, he will. But you should hear him out.' "

"You'll go away forever?" Stephanie said.

Howdy sighed. "I'll do it," he said. "You follow my MG out to the house and wait at the end of the drive while I make your pitch for you. But what are you going to say to Maureen to convince her and make her change?"

"I don't know," Chris said. "I don't have any idea."

"The bugs are all excited," Stephanie said.

"What are you saying, sweetheart?" Howdy said.

"I hate 'sweetheart,' Howdy. It looks like the bugs and birds are all jittery. The crickets are singing in the middle of daylight."

"Might be a storm," Chris said.

Stephanie said, "But it's clear in the sky, though. There's not even a breeze."

"Settle down, I believe you," Howdy said.

11

Cleveland draped his work clothes on the hamper. He stepped into the shower stall. He weaved a bit, letting the spray pound his back. When he could move again, he got out and used a towel to buff a face-sized patch in the mirror. A glass of vodka, made pale yellow by a little orange juice, stood next to his nickel-plated safety razor. Without bothering to lather his jaws or to consult the mirror very often, he tied the towel around his neck and shaved. He drank too much of the vodka, coughed, shivered, and took the glass into his bedroom.

Brigitte Bardot, pouty-lipped at twenty and with loosely piled hair, was on the screen of his red portable television set. Holding his towel over his hips with a fist, Cleveland struggled for balance and watched.

Maureen came into the bedroom after rapping on the open door. She looked at her father, looked away, and walked out.

"It's nearly one o'clock, for Christ's sake!" Cleveland shouted at her. "Get out of that G-string and into some clothes!"

"Never mind!" Maureen called back from down the hall.

Cleveland dressed in featherweight slacks and an electric yellow shirt trimmed with a green collar. He put on a leather slipper, his watch, and a gold neckchain. He buttoned the throat of his shirt. He searched the corners of the carpet for his second slipper. He filled up his baggy trouser pockets with a folding wallet, keys on a ring, a Swiss Army knife, and—after using it to mop his wet, browned face—a linen hanky. Without meaning to, he moved suddenly backward. His legs banged against the bed and he sat down. Rushes of alcohol-generated heat ascended from his stomach to his chest.

A French Army officer talked huskily to Brigitte Bardot. A dubbed-in voice answered for her. The picture flipped twice and died, and then a banner of white letters crossed the screen. Cleveland leaned forward to read them. But he could not make them out. A voice announced, "This is a weather bulletin from Channel Five meteorologist Stan Manley and the Weather Bureau. Stand by, please."

"I can't stand by," Cleveland said. "I'm going to sit by."

"There is a tornado watch in effect until three this afternoon, for Ventig, Rahway, and Miggs counties. The National Weather Service reports sightings of funnel clouds in northern Miggs County. Residents are advised . . ."

Violet strolled into the bedroom in fresh clothes and dived onto the bed, accidentally kicking Cleveland.

"I'm listening," Cleveland said.

"To what?"

The TV voice repeated, "The National Weather Service has issued a tornado watch for Ventig . . ."

"Weather," Cleveland said. "This is bad weather, but it's far away. I wanted to hear if it's coming. But I didn't hear. It's your fault."

Violet said, "Mom told me to tell you Birginia's here."

"Say Vurr," Cleveland said.

"Burr."

Cleveland rocked on his bottom, building momentum for an attempt to stand. He pushed up. "What's your name?" he said. He walked a straight line to the TV and tapped the on-off knob.

"Violet."

"Good. Now, who's coming to visit? And don't be cute." He yanked the drawers on the chest, rummaged in one of them, found a paisley scarf, and stuffed it around his neck. "Old man's got to wear a sweat rag these days," he said. "Say Vurr, vurr, vurr."

"Virginia," Violet said.

"That's right. Home of Robert E. Lee and Smithfield hams. You know who you look like, Violet? You look like Brigitte Bardot."

"Did I hear something about a hurricane?" Maureen said at the bedroom door.

"Did I hear something about Virginia being here?" Cleveland said.

"Yeah, a minute ago. Dad, it's freezing in this house, or haven't you noticed?"

"You're cold because you're wet and naked. I'm hot, so the air conditioner stays on. Aren't you ever going to get dressed?"

"When you tell me if we're going to have a storm or not," Maureen said.

"There're some bad clouds," Cleveland said, "but they're south of us." He bared his teeth in an ugly grimace. "Ouch," he said. "My God!" he said, and rubbed his stomach.

"I knew this was coming," Maureen said. "You'll be in bed for a week from that gin."

"Vodka. Violet, tell Virginia I'll be right down. Tell her to make herself a drink."

"I'll get your antacid," Maureen said. "Do what he says, Vi."

"And get dressed," Cleveland said, trying to focus on his daughter's face.

12

Earlier, in the morning, after his breakfast of screwdrivers and a sweet roll, Cleveland had met his gardener, Jack, who was already pissed to the gills. Jack had a post-hole digger on the bed of his pickup. The digger had a top-mounted engine the size of an outboard motor. There were opposing handles on the engine, and the two men had gripped the handles and, standing on the ridge of the ravine, worked to bore a hole into dirt that was baked stone-hard. The digger had fought them, had bucked and danced, wrenching them right and left. Its screw blades, after going only inches deep, had slammed into rock and made the big engine jerk, spin, throw the two men down.

From this position, Cleveland had said, "I'm too looped for this." He had pulled off his orange work gloves. "Let's hose down these holes, soak them all night with water, and hang it up for today."

That was when he had closed off the house, switched on the air conditioning, and set the thermostat at fifty degrees.

13

The cooling system made a noise. Maureen listened, sitting alone on Violet's bed, her long arms around one of Violet's stuffed dogs. She tried rubbing the gooseflesh off her thighs. She opened Violet's window for some of the warmth of the day, and noticed a commotion in the still and windless yard. Birds were crying. Sparrows were hectoring a jay, diving at it, chattering threats. There was a strange tan cast to the visible southern sky.

She experienced a sudden, restless sort of depression. She found herself examining her hands, which were bulky with painted square fingernails and prominent mannish veins. She took a fingernail between her teeth and bit off too much. She stuck the finger in her mouth, caressed the sore place with the end of her tongue. She studied a tack hole in the wall. She called sharply for Violet.

The child came, nibbling a frozen Milky Way. Maureen put her on the bed and told her, "I want you to come up and keep me company while I get dressed. I'm going to wear the new dress that I was saving. Then, when I'm dressed, we're going to go out there and I'm going to talk to whoever will listen to me and talk back."

"Why, Mom? What's wrong?" Violet said. "Why do I have to sit with you?"

Something awful was closing down on Maureen. Her stomach had dropped as if it had someplace lower to go. She stood waiting, holding her breath. She exhaled with a whimper. "I'm not giving in to this," she said. "I'm proceeding on. Come help me change." She took Violet's hand and marched her down the hall and up the wide staircase to the second floor.

"What do I do with this candy wrapper?" Violet said.

In her bedroom, Maureen took the candy wrapper and put it under her pillow. She felt better—until she glimpsed her reflection in the mirror. Her pupils were dilated and she thought she saw a rash on her face.

"Violet? Does my face look funny?"

Violet didn't answer.

"Tell me," Maureen said. "It's okay if you tell me."

"It's red," Violet said.

"What's red about it?" Maureen said, and moved closer to the mirror. She saw the spider web of broken blood vessels spun across her nose and cheekbones.

"I think it's sunburn," Violet said.

"What about my eyes?" Maureen kneeled in front of Violet. "No, hold it. Maybe I just got moisturizer in them."

"They're fine," Violet said.

Maureen stood up. She put on sunglasses and started a record on her stereo. "Wanna dance?" she said to Violet.

"No, I really don't."

"I have to turn it off, anyway," Maureen said. "As much as it helps me, Uncle Howdy always says it's a bad idea to get dressed to music. You're likely to jump out of your clothes." Maureen had removed her bikini and was trying on underwear. She put a strapless bra on, inhaled deeply, and the bra fell off. "Oh, damn. There go the eyehooks, and that's the only bra I have for under a sundress."

"You can fix it," Violet said.

"No," Maureen said. "Not so it'll ever look right. Let me see. I'll just go without."

She stepped into a dress with a pattern of red and green confetti. "One thing would be deadly," she said, "and that's for me to lie down. If I did that, I'd lie there and I'd be lost. I must go outside myself. It's a trick, but I've done it before."

"I know," Violet said.

"Let's go get Virginia talking. I have things to tell her that'll stop me from thinking about myself."

"Aren't you going to wear shoes?" Violet said.

Maureen looked at her feet a while. She said, "Goddamn you, Vi. Now I can't decide. What am I supposed to do? Wear shoes or not?"

Violet shrugged. "You look pretty."

"You think I do?" Maureen said, amazed. "You've never said anything like that before. Why would you say that, Violet? It's so nice!" She crouched in front of her daughter, but the attention went out of Violet's eyes. Maureen said, "Violet, where are you? Can you hear me?"

"Of course I hear you," Violet said. "I'm just looking at myself in your glasses."

Maureen sighed and got comfortable on her knees. She said, "You know what's funny? I used to think my mother was pretty, too. It was a pleasure to be seen with her. Except for Howdy, I was the happiest child I've ever known. I was so proud! I knew all Mom's dresses, and had particular favorites —her black and white polka dot, that was the best." She held Violet close, but Violet said, "Stop," and ran away.

Lola banged past on some errand, talking to herself.

14

Virginia was decked out in a golfish wraparound skirt, immaculate sneakers, and a polo top. She gestured and laughed from one end of the sofa, and capped the point of her crossed knee with her white canvas hat. She pushed the telling of her anecdote as Violet sprinted at her. "So there I was, with a thimble on my finger, sewing on this mysterious jacket—all for the little dog I used to have—Dante.

"Hello, dear," she said to Violet.

Maureen slouched a little, sabotaging the effect of entering in a new dress. She crossed the living room and said, "Hey, girl," to Stephanie, who had been listening to Virginia from the brick ledge that jutted from the fireplace. Stephanie got up and, along with Virginia, made a fuss about Maureen's dress and even about the old, open-toed shoes Maureen had chosen. Maureen sat, embarrassed, with her leg hooked over the arm of a stuffed chair. She did and undid a button at the throat of her dress.

"Howdy's got to talk to you," Stephanie said. She reached down and tugged some burrs from the cuff of her pants.

"Is that Maureen?" Howdy's voice said from the kitchen. "I need to talk to you!"

"All right, I got the message!" Maureen yelled. "Howdy? Could you bring me a beer or something?"

"And a Coke!" Violet yelled.

"Get it yourself, Violet," Maureen said. "You're a big girl."

"Right!" Howdy yelled. "A Coke and a Scotch sour! A Scotch sour, Maureen? I'm making a blenderful!"

Virginia said, "You folks need an intercom, like I have at my place."

Stephanie said, "How about walkie-talkies?"

"Yeah!" Violet said.

Maureen said, "Violet, in the bathroom cabinet in your bathroom is a pouch with Mommy's nail stuff. Would you be a big girl and run get it for me? Also, I left my cigarettes and lighter in your room."

"No," Violet said.

"Mercy, it's chilly in here," Virginia said. "When Violet let me in, she told me her grandad is feeling ill and wants it this cold. Is that correct? Is he ill?"

"He's okay," Maureen said. "He'll be joining us any minute."

"He hasn't been drinking, has he?" Virginia said.

"Not so you'd notice," Maureen said. "Except maybe you would. But, hell, Virginia, who am I to tell you about Dad's stamina?"

"Oh, I don't know," Virginia said.

"You know how it is once men start to go. Dad can work a garden, sure," Maureen said. "Fix lights and plumbing sometimes. But the cumulative effects show when he's trying to do something like recall a phone number. And his good-time days are over. For the most part, he's a broken-down man who only gets things done because he has to. But if he's up late on Monday, then Tuesday he'll go to sleep right after the seven o'clock news. And that doesn't include his after-lunch naps and the naps he falls into all day long right in the middle of sentences. Violet, do your grandpa imitation."

Violet got up from the sofa. "Okay," she said, "here's how Grandpa goes. He goes—" Violet let her head roll slowly sideways and her eyes slide shut. She snapped up to straight-spined attention and said, "I'm awake, I'm awake," then sagged and repeated the head roll.

"Hey, that's great!" Stephanie said and applauded.

Virginia touched Violet's arm. "Your grandfather could teach many a younger man a world of things. About manners, about decency, about kindness to your neighbor. And never to go where you're not welcome—forcing your way in. And about being gentle and wise, and having good, strong spiritual roots. People need roots, Violet, like trees need roots, or they get dry and dead and blow around in the wind like tumble-weeds. Would you excuse me, all of you? I want to see how he's doing." Virginia raised herself from the sofa and left them, eddies of Shalimar stirring in her passage.

"So there, Maureen!" Maureen said.

"What?" Stephanie said. "Was Virginia mad?"

Maureen said, "Are you really planning to marry my half-wit brother?"

Stephanie giggled and spoke to some freckles on her fore-arm. "Oh, Howdy loves to talk. He likes to tell people things."

"Violet, go get my nail polish and cigarettes right now or you'll be grounded, and I'm serious." Violet dragged herself away. Maureen went over to Stephanie and sat beside her on the hearth. Out in the kitchen, the blender sang.

"I'm really cold," Stephanie said. "Look at my blue fingernails."

"Never mind," Maureen said. "I was saying, when it comes to Howdy, you know, it's a slow week if he doesn't propose marriage to at least two imbeciles of any gender."

"Really?" Stephanie said, and giggled some more.

"No, not really," Maureen said. "If nothing else, Howdy's sincere. And I can tell that you're not going to marry him. The poor, luckless dope. I wonder, did you ever sleep together?"

"Oh, sure, sure." Stephanie giggled and nodded.

"You really have?"

"Yeah. How come you asked?"

"Just dumb," Maureen said, and went back to her chair.

Violet returned and dropped off the nail-kit bag and cigarettes. "Can I go outside and play in the wind?"

Maureen tapped a cigarette from the fat blue pack and dragged on it discontentedly. She looked out the glass doors where, beyond the veranda, the landscape was being rushed at by dark, irritable clouds. She could not hear the wind, but saw it twisting tree branches, turning leaves over onto their light side. She said, "Yes, I guess you can go out. But stay close to the house and stay out from under trees and come back the second it starts to rain. And don't go around the power tools." She snapped on the table lamp beside her chair.

When Violet went out through the sliding glass doors, Maureen noticed the wind, loud enough to hear over the air conditioner.

Howdy carried in a tray loaded with drinks on coasters. He was shivering a little in a snap-tab shirt. He served Stephanie and Maureen where they sat, and put the tray down on the coffee table. He said, "This whole family drinks too much in the summer. You'd better get used to it, Steph, seeing as how you're already one of the family."

"My dad drinks more," Stephanie said.

"And he can handle them," Howdy said. "What are you staring at me for, Mo? Is my hair on backwards?"

"Just thinking," Maureen said.

"Well, tell us about what, because then I have to talk to you," Howdy said. He looked out the sliding doors. "Jesus, is it blowing! Poor anybody who's out there and not in this cold house."

"I love this house," Maureen said. "Except for that little bit with Chris, I've never lived anyplace else. I couldn't be comfortable or feel safe anywhere else, could you?"

"Hurry up," Howdy said.

"Yet I don't want to be stuck here the rest of my life," Maureen said. "Except I'm scared of going anywhere else. Of living out my days being poor. Probably with Chris around."

Howdy looked at Stephanie. He said, "Maureen, why would Chris be around?"

"I don't know," Maureen said. "But from now on, wherever I go, I know he'll be there."

"But what's so bad about that? He seems all right to me," Howdy said.

"I think Chris is cute," Stephanie said.

"Now, now," Maureen said, and dropped back into her chair. She pulled one last time on her cigarette, then punched it out in the ashtray. "Those are good drinks. I mean really good."

"Aren't they?" Howdy said. He went around the room, tripped a wall switch that put on a track of lights over the fireplace and a spotlight recessed into the ceiling and trained on the sofa. He turned on the television. He said, "I like this—everybody praising my drinks. Let's get the word on the storm. Steph, will you watch for a bulletin while I talk privately to my sister?"

15

Violet had gone from the veranda into the yard at the side of the house. The southern horizon just over the trees that lined Charity Way was jet shading to khaki. There were low, dirty clouds with monstrous furrowed bottoms. The child made a dash for the toolshed, where she found her roller skates—white ankle-highs—on the seat of a small tractor. She took the skates outside to tie them on, afraid of the wolf spiders that lived in the shed. When she had laced and knotted one skate, she lay on her back. The clouds streamed overhead, their bulky bellies lined with black ditches, some tearing apart, pieces coming loose and spinning away.

With both skates in place, Violet clomped up the lawn, crossed back over the veranda, and came out by a plot of flower garden—wands of periwinkles, waving sweet williams, and expiring phlox—behind the new garage.

"Hey, champ!" Lola called, leaning out an upstairs window. Her head was turbaned in red. She folded her arms on the sill.

"Lola, it's night over there," Violet said, and pointed south.

"Radio says we're going to have a twister," Lola said. "So don't go anywhere."

"Twister?" Violet's hair whipped her face.

"Like Dorothy had in *The Wizard of Oz.*"

Violet hobbled on, balancing as she rolled past a pile of oil cans and fuming rags, metal shears, a calendar, a moldy box of books topped by Zane Grey and *Forever Amber.* She built up speed and zoomed out onto the Cleveland drive. She passed the bronze nymph in the arbor, rounded the corner there nicely, and came onto the lane proper. She had stopped pumping and was coasting just before she hit a pothole, flew into the air, and skidded down on her stomach, her chin cracking the pavement.

She blinked lights and stars, but got right up, and making great sniffling sounds, she trudged back toward the house—walking more than rolling.

16

Thirty yards from the evergreens at the drive's entrance gate, an old elm creaked from the weight of the truck tire tied high in the swaying tree. Chris was riding the tree.

"Baby!" he said, the weather almost swallowing his voice. He hopped down and jogged for her in a comic crouch, then did a neat forward roll and plunked onto the seat of his chinos in time to wrap her in his arms.

"I lost my balance and hit my head," Violet said. "Is my chin bloody?"

"No, no, you're fine," Chris said, looking at her through dark glasses that had fogged over in the wet wind. They rolled together on the lawn, clumsily because of Violet's skates.

"I'll wager they sent you to get me. Did they?"

"No, but Dad, will you look at my face? Does it look funny? I was going along and there was a hole."

"You're fine. Wonderful. Unmarked. But wait a minute, you say they *didn't* send you to bring me back?"

Violet shook her head.

"I'll be damned," Chris shouted. "And you're just out here on roller skates? They let you skate around in this catastrophe?"

"It's okay," Violet shouted back.

"Listen, Vi, this is important. Howdy was supposed to talk to Mommy for me. Was he talking to Mommy? Was Howdy doing that?"

"Howdy was in the kitchen."

"That's a good sign," Chris said. "Now you come with me

to my car. If we don't get inside somewhere, we're going to get blown away."

Violet said, "Not with my skates on, I won't."

Chris's car was on the shoulder of Charity Way, tucked into some spiraea shrubs. Violet got into the jump seat and inspected the tools Chris kept back there in a wooden box. She tipped the carpenter's level. She drew on her hand with the grease pencil. She tore a blueprint into bits and let them fly from the window.

Chris made a steeple with his fingers. He said, "Howdy has five minutes and then I make my move. In five minutes, I hit the goddamn beach."

17

Maureen was furious. She was also drunk. She took some punches at the furniture, landed left hooks and right crosses on the couch.

"Are you finished, do you think?" Howdy said.

"Howdy, you're so fucking dumb. How did I get such an asinine brother? Always stumbling around in some half-lit world."

"All right, I'm dumb," Howdy said. "Now deal with the question."

"Get fucked," Maureen said.

Stephanie excused herself and went for the hall bathroom.

"I saw what you did to the hedges!" Maureen yelled after her.

Howdy said, "Just let me know when you're all through, Mo."

"How could you live here and be around me all the time and not know what Chris does to me? How could you let him invade the sanctity of this house? And expose him to Violet?

Don't you know how smart he is? How smart he *really* is? He fools you because he can act so reasonable and make such sense. I can't believe he suckered you, Howdy, when you should really remember this stuff."

"Just let me know when you're done."

"Idiot!" Maureen yelled.

Howdy looked at his folded arms and elbows, pretending patience. "Now, listen," he said. "Maybe the problem is I don't know Chris the way you do. But I don't frankly know why he makes you so insane. All right, so he does. Believe me, I can see that he does. But please understand that this was supposed to be doing you a favor."

"Say no more to me," Maureen said.

"Will you wait a minute?" Howdy said. "And hear what I'm trying to say? We'll stay in the room with you, Steph and me. We'll all listen to whatever Chris is going to say. He'll get twenty minutes, no more. Then he goes—forever—just the way he promised. You get rid of him forever, Mo."

"Oh, I believe that," Maureen said.

"He swore. In front of witnesses."

"You pathetic asshole," Maureen said.

"I gotta tell you, Mo, I've never heard you talk like this. To tell you the truth, it's a little frightening."

Maureen dumped herself down in a chair, her full skirt floating up over her thighs nearly to her underpants. She yawned and said, "I'm frightening? Is that what you're saying? I'm frightening?"

Howdy turned away. He said, "Hey, Mo, could you cover yourself up and button your blouse and quit playing the drunken floozy? Because if you go on talking and acting like you've been doing, Dad'll come out here and say you shouldn't be allowed to drink anymore. Besides, we learned in acting workshop that truly drunk people make an enormous effort to act normal. I mean, you can tell they're drunk because they're overly prim and cautious, which is what a *good* actor does."

Maureen said, "*Acting* workshop! Really, Howdy, if I were you, I swear I'd kill myself."

"I'm just a person trying," Howdy said. He took a small sip from his drink and settled the glass back on a table. "And the guy I had for that class was a real authority. Christ, he'd been a chess partner of Arthur Miller's. Anyway, Mo, maybe this isn't the time to say this, but I've been thinking."

"Please," she said, "you're going to make me laugh and I don't want to."

"I've got this idea," Howdy said, ignoring her. "I started thinking about it last spring and it just stays with me. I'm going to Ireland. I've decided I'm going to Ireland to see Mother."

"I know, I know. You and Stephanie are going on a bicycle ride around Europe."

"Skip Europe," Howdy said, raising both his hands to wipe everything aside. "Don't you want to see your own mother? I always thought, when I was a kid, that she was—like, you know, unreachable. And then I realized, hell, she's just in *Ireland*, for crying out loud."

Maureen arranged her dress and straightened her posture.

"So why don't you and I go see her?" Howdy said. "What'd be so wrong with that? She'd be uncomfortable at first. So would we. But then we'd go to the theater or dinner and we'd all loosen up. She probably misses us. She's probably ashamed and guilty. And we could both just say, 'It's all right, Mother, we're okay, we love you and you're forgiven.' "

After a long moment, Maureen said, "We ought to go for her sake if for no other reason. We could let her off the hook about us. All we'd really want to do is kind of be friends with her. She's getting old by now. There's no guarantee she'll be around forever."

"True," Howdy said.

"Showing Violet to Mom would be good, letting Violet meet her grandmother."

"Right!" Howdy said. "And this Chris thing, it was just to close that chapter for you, once and for all, Maureen. It's something we're all dreading, but then you can move on. After today, if he shows up again, we'll just have him arrested. See, the thing is, Mo, since I've known Steph, I feel I can do anything. My only problem is finding what's most important to do."

"Mother," Maureen said.

18

Something pushed against the flanks of Chris's car, rocking it. "My God, is this the end of the world?" he said. He picked up Violet's hand and held it a minute.

"Can't we go?" she said.

"Let's just sit and talk awhile. How've you been, hon? I saw something interesting on the way over here. I saw this woman with a shaved head."

Violet said, "Can we go in, Dad? I got hiccups and I need a glass of water." She held up her stubby index finger, signaling for him to listen, and then she hiccuped twice.

"We can fix you, Vi. Look at me. Don't laugh. Take a deep, deep breath."

"I'm doing it," Violet said in a voice from the base of her throat.

Chris waited. He brought from the wing of his blazer a cardboard folder of Hava Tampa Jewels and a wallet-sized bottle of Johnny Walker—Black. "Hello, John. My name's Chris," Chris said. He uncapped the bottle and drank. He lit a cigar. "Let go of your breath now, baby."

She wagged her head no.

"You really better. You're turning colors. No? Another

thing I saw on the way over, just in passing—this was a woman sitting on top of a wrecked car. I mean it, no kidding, Violet, you really better let go."

Violet forced another ten seconds before she exhaled.

"All right," Chris said, "it's thirty-one hundred hours or twelve o'clock high. Do I look handsome enough for your mom?" He punched open the glove compartment and lifted out a shard of mirror. He ran it in the air in front of his face. He fluffed his hair.

"Not that way," Violet told him. She pressed a wave against his temple. "Ooh, gross," she said, as her wrist brushed the stubble on his jaw.

"I look splendid," he said. "Thanks." He showed her a front view. Violet fixed his hair some more.

"Is that really better?" He checked his reflection.

"Make your bangs lay down."

Chris patted his forehead. "Okay?"

"There!" Violet said.

"It's now or never," Chris said.

They got out of the car, and he pulled her through the wind toward the house. At the door, he threw his cigar into the shrubbery before he rang the bell.

19

Goodness," Maureen said. She was watching the television. Brigitte Bardot's bare back was to the camera. She had dropped her bed sheet and was standing naked for several actors in Nazi uniforms. "My heavens," Maureen said. "Hello, Chris. Do come in. You'll like this on TV."

"Stephanie, Howdy, Maureen," Chris said. He tossed them all a nervous salute. Behind him, Violet jangled on her skates.

"Can they *show* this?" Maureen said, her speech noticeably slurred. "Isn't that her backside?"

Howdy and Stephanie left their places on the hearth and came around for a better view of the screen. Chris squinted. He was only a little way into the room. There was a cut in the movie to some partisans stuffing TNT under a railroad tie. Everyone watched through the next scene, and then the next. Then a ribbon of white words moved across the bottom of the picture.

"There is a tornado warning in effect for Rope County," Howdy read aloud.

"That's us, Violet," Maureen said. "We're Rope." Howdy shushed her. They heard that part of the tornado had touched down to the south of them, knocking hell out of a block of homes.

"What we need is more drinks," Maureen said.

"I like this," Stephanie said. "If it weren't so cold."

"No, honey, you don't," Howdy said. He shook his head. "Some people were killed from it already."

"The cold feels good to me," Chris said. "Many's the day I've stood around grocery stores at the freezers just for the good old cold."

"Do we go to the basement?" Maureen said.

"I think I've heard the bathroom is best," Chris said.

"It'd be crowded if we all go to the bathroom," Stephanie said.

Violet was on the floor, picking at the knots in her skate laces. She gave up and went to the kitchen. Maureen could hear her rolling on the linoleum.

"Don't hang around on the shore of the carpet, Chris," Maureen said. "And, Howdy, why don't you mix more drinks so Chris can have one."

Chris said, "Where should I be that wouldn't make you nervous? Just say where I should be, Mo."

"Not by the damned door," she said.

Howdy led Stephanie out. Chris lowered himself onto the ottoman in front of Maureen's chair. "Thank you for letting me in," he said.

"Yeah, fine," Maureen said.

"May I tell you how great you look in that dress?"

"Yes."

"I was supposed to have all this stuff to say to you," Chris said.

"You know, you *are* cute," Maureen said.

"So are you," Chris said.

"Stand up." They both got up and Maureen fitted herself against him. She dipped her head and wetly kissed his throat.

"Man," he said. "Lord."

She gave him a sleepy smile. "So where did you catch Violet?"

"On the drive out there. She'd just done a somersault and smacked her chin. But she's perfectly okay. Can we go somewhere private?"

"And waste your time? You've only got about fourteen minutes left."

Chris turned his back.

Violet appeared with a cereal bowl. "Please go, Violet," Chris said.

Violet looked at her mother, who said, "You don't have to, Vi. Just promise you'll be quiet."

Chris said, "Please, for *me*."

Violet went to the TV and sat in front of the screen, her legs bracketing her bowl of cereal.

"This," Chris said, through locked teeth, "is the most control you'll ever see anyone exhibit. And only because you're crocked, Mo. See? I'm not going to do either of the two things my body screams for me to do. I'm not going to."

"Settle down," Maureen said.

"A big, big part of me wants to crumple at your feet—believe it or not—under the soles of your shoes."

"For sex," Maureen said.

"For love," he said.

"Oh, shut up," she said. "You know I'm not against sex. Sex is all right. True, it's a lot of bother. It just means work—new underwear all the time, special perfume, legs perfectly shaved. When someone suggests an affair to me, I just think work."

"Like who?" Chris said.

"Lay off, will you?" Maureen said.

"And the other thing I want to do is give you a short, devastating left hook in the stomach."

"Vi, go help your uncle," Maureen said.

Violet didn't move.

"Violet!" Maureen screeched.

"All right, Mom, I'm going. God!"

When she was gone, Maureen said, "You belong in prison. You're violent. You're crazy. You broke teeth."

"I chipped one tooth," Chris said. "And you drove me to it. No sane human being could have done otherwise."

"It's my fault that someone acts like a savage? I don't care what you say, no man should ever hit. If he can't stop himself, he ought to be locked up for the rest of his life."

"What are you doing to me?" Chris screamed. "I came here to plead with you. How did you get this turned around?"

"Mo?" Howdy called from the kitchen.

"It's all right," she called back.

"Thank you," Chris said. "Bless you for that."

"Hmph," Maureen said. "I'm just not afraid of you anymore. I'm fucking numb. I hope you hit me, so you can go to the penitentiary. Anyway, I'm going away to live with my mother in Ireland and I'm taking Violet. So I really don't care what you do. Go ahead and bash me one. God forbid you should leave without getting your kicks."

"Oh, that's so stupid it takes the anger right out of me," Chris said. "Thank you for that stupidity. Howdy! How are those drinks shaking up?"

"In a minute!" Howdy called back.

"Listen," Chris said. "I came here to say I really want to try living with you again. I need to see my daughter more than every once in a while. I'll do anything you say—whatever you say. I'll tag along to Ireland or wherever, and I won't touch you." He held up both hands. "I'll work hard to support you."

"Maybe I was believing you until you said that."

Chris said, "Would it mean anything if I told you I don't see anyone else? Not ever? That's proof, isn't it?"

"It would mean something if I believed you," Maureen said. "But I don't."

20

Virginia said, "Are you better now?"

"Just want to sit," Cleveland said.

"Then sit we shall," Virginia said.

"The deck has stopped tilting, but the wallpaper's still falling on me," Cleveland said. "This is no goddamn way to feel. I got a big fire in my gut."

"Maureen says you're getting fragile, wearing down." Virginia lowered her voice. "I felt like telling her just how robust her father is."

Cleveland sat up stiffly.

"Poor old bird," Virginia said, embracing him and rocking him back and forth on the bed.

"I'll live. I'd sure hate to miss you being sweet. I'm in a big mess, aren't I?"

"Are you unhappy?"

"I'm settling down. The worst is over," Cleveland said.

"Shall we tell them tonight? When you're feeling better? About the twentieth?"

"Don't care," he said.

"May I look at the piano room while you rest? I need to get an idea of space."

"Have at it," Cleveland said.

She propped her chin on his shoulder. "Poor old bean. You just want to be left alone and here I am cuddling you, driving you nuts. Can I bring you anything?"

"Sorry. Really sorry." Cleveland lay back on the bed. "Don't move too fast, is all."

Virginia got a washcloth from the bathroom, soaked it with cold water, and squeezed it out. She put the cloth on Cleveland's head and went down the hallway and up the stairs.

21

Lola had almost finished with the entire second floor. She had wiped the windows and the French doors, vacuumed, dusted, sent out the heavy old draperies and hung clean muslin ones for summer. She had rolled up the scatter rugs and put down straw mats, swept out the fireplace in the piano room, changed the candles in the pewter sticks for fresh ones, oiled and polished the two highboys. She carried an Amish quilt—one that usually hung flat on the far wall of the piano room—out onto the west balcony and fought for the quilt with the wind.

"You're getting help flapping that out!" Virginia shouted from inside.

Lola pulled the quilt down and gathered it into a bundle against her chest. She stepped off the balcony, closed and latched the French doors. "Thought that wind was going to yank me off the roof."

"I'll bet it blew the dust from that blanket," Virginia said.

Lola stood on a chair, took a little hammer and tacks from her smock, and rehung the quilt.

"That's perfect. What a lovely thing. It must be two hundred years old," Virginia said.

"My age exactly," Lola said.

"Isn't this nice?" Virginia said. She had picked up a ceramic tiger from a table beside the love seat. "So many fine things here."

Lola's radio—a purse-sized plastic box with an antenna, a padded handle, and an eight-track cassette-player—was tuned to a jazz station. Someone was bluntly chording on a piano. The music was staccato, disruptive, repetitious. Lola winced and rolled the tuner knob. She settled on a news report long enough to hear an interview with a woman who had seen the roof of her house blasted off by the tornado. The woman's television set had attacked her, she said, jumped across the room to get her. "The cat blowed all around in circles. Things come flying from every which where. My husband grabs me. Our Janet flies in from the kitchen and rams the wall and she's only seventeen! Broke her arm, it did. Sounds just like we got a great big train going over. I can't even hear you yet, my ears is dead-like."

Virginia was counting the electrical outlets. "I never understood what they expect you to do when weather's on the way. But listening to her, I couldn't help wondering how any thinking person can deny the existence of God."

"She was lucky. That's true," Lola said.

"It just stops you in your tracks. Something had to be watching her."

"I hope it's watching us," Lola said.

"Well, it's out of our hands. I find that comforting in a way, don't you?" Virginia said.

"I guess," Lola said.

"Are there only two outlets in this room?"

"That's it," Lola said. "The boss put in new everything when he renovated the place and added the garage and new wings and all. But one thing he didn't do is add outlets up here."

"As often as they let you down," Virginia said, "men are still capable of doing thrilling things—the right men."

Lola leaned her back against the mantelpiece. She said, "The boss got it for his wife—Howdy's and Mo's mom. She was from the British Isles and homesick as hell, so this place was supposed to fix that for her. He's said he doesn't think she'd have married him or stayed ten minutes if it weren't for this place. She could pretend she was Lady La-Di-Da and mistress of the manor and that he wasn't a hillbilly boy but a bluenose, too. The boss told me he used to go around in riding pants and a smoking jacket, chewing on a pipe."

"God bless him. Can't you see it?" Virginia said. "I understand she was a very distraught woman. Perhaps an alcoholic or deranged."

"That makes sense," Lola said. "But if you want to keep your good looks, don't ever say it around Howdy or Maureen."

Virginia focused on a standing lamp with a parchment shade. She didn't seem to have heard.

22

Chris had talked Maureen onto the brick veranda. She stretched in a vinyl and aluminum chaise. He sat backwards on a cast-iron chair, and ran his finger around the tracery of the chair's leafy pattern. "I've done this all wrong," he said. "I shouldn't have groveled. It's unappealing. I've had no pride."

"How eerie," Maureen said, looking up. The wind had died and, in the calm, the light was beige. "I can't locate the sun." Sooty clouds swarmed, billowed, tore apart, but without the sound track of the wind. Brilliant splinters of lightning ignited from cloud to cloud, yet there was no report. "Whew! It's like the overture's finished and the curtain's about to go up."

"You know what I think?" Chris said, his face caught in a stare. "I think when I won that lottery I used up all the luck I'll ever have."

"That's occurred to me," Maureen said. "You also used up your twenty minutes."

"Give me two more minutes," Chris said.

"I knew it. Got a light?"

He said, "Maureen? Who gave you so much liquor? You know when you get squashed you throw up."

"I used to be that way. I'm not that way anymore. I'm this way. But here's Chris, everybody, dragging a tornado with him. We're all so happy to see you."

"Could I have my lighter back, please? Guilt? Is that what I inspire in you?"

"You are the past," she said. "I hate it. I don't even want one. My past is a joke. Violet—there's one joke. She gets under everyone's feet and she reminds them that I, Maureen, am a twenty-four-year-old failure. What are you looking at?" Her legs opened as she twisted in the chair.

Chris's eyes went back and forth, from the high, sun-tanned insides of her thighs to a white shape in the sky that was revolving and reaching for the ground. The funnel was half a mile up, rumbling enormously. Hailstones flew crossways, like pellets shot from a gun.

23

The storm was quick and spectacular. It passed them violently on the east, but no funnel cloud touched down, no damage was done. A heavy, friendly rain followed, from clouds so thickly massed they made a false twilight.

Maureen had taken Violet down to the cellar and snuggled with her under a pedestal table. They had dug into a steamer trunk that had ten years' worth of family stuff. They had played a few hands of a simple card game Violet knew. Howdy and Chris had gone out into the yard and gotten soaked watching. Stephanie, Lola, and Virginia had lined up on the couch and more or less ignored a daytime TV drama. Cleveland had slept through it all.

"Could we turn down the damn air conditioning now?" Howdy said. "I can see everybody's breath." He was shivering in his seat on a blue and burgundy runner at the front of the living room. Rain dripped from his flattened hair, from his ears and nose, shirt and pants.

"Your father gave me strict orders that I wouldn't let that be done," Virginia said.

"Mr. Cleveland says it's healthy to be chilled when you're drunk," Lola said. "He told me it stabilizes all the heat your body makes from the liquor." She had left the couch and slumped into a Sheraton chair by the hearth, drinking stout from a frosted bottle.

"It *is* healthy," said Chris, as he got down on the floor next to Howdy. "Pneumonia's the best thing in the summer months to combat any dangerous urges to exercise or eat well or be sober." Chris drank his third straight whiskey. "Hey, come on," he said to the silent room. "That was just trying to be funny." He elbowed Howdy. "An attempt at humor."

"I've got a tongue twister," Virginia said, "that I made up. Super-zipper-duffel-bag."

Maureen said, "Super-zipper-duffel-bag, super-zipper-duffel-bag, super-zipper-duffel-bag. Big deal." She said, "Tell us, Virginia. Should we be grateful to God for sparing us, for not having us thrown around and killed by the tornado, or should we be annoyed at him for sending it down in the first place?"

"If you're serious and not teasing, I'll tell you what I think," Virginia said. She had borrowed a cardigan from Lola and was hugging herself with it. "I think that how you feel is *your* business, and you—I mean, one—should probably try to feel whatever makes you most happy."

"No argument in that," Lola said.

Maureen said, "But according to you, Virginia, why does God test us all the time with fires and floods and famines and diseases? If a god made us and loves us, then why does he give us grief with stuff like cancer and deformed children?"

"The profundity of the soused," Howdy said.

"I'm not soused yet," Maureen said. "I was just thinking that if Violet treated her gerbil the way God treats us—like cutting off its arms and blinding it just to test if the thing had faith or not—then we'd be furious. And I just wonder what the fuck we did that we deserve to have our brains screwed out by a tornado."

"I think Violet did indeed kill that gerbil," Howdy said. "But that's immaterial. I always believed the junk about living by the sword, then dying by the sword. And if your life is like a tornado in many ways, Maureen, then there you go. That's what you get. Just based on what I know of your life, I'd've been terrified of that storm."

"That is superstitious assholeness," Maureen said.

"Take it or leave it," Howdy said.

Maureen fetched herself a fresh drink.

"We're all weary," Virginia said. "It's making us say foolish things. Something about the sameness of the summer days is fatiguing us."

Lola said, "I put it in a poem for Professor Riley's class. I wrote: 'I awaken to the scorching heat and wonder where the days are going. But oh how blue is that August sky.' "

"Bravo!" Chris said.

"What's the matter with all of you?" Maureen said. "You're talking about sameness? We were just nearly stamped out by a merciless act of nature."

"Tornadoes are pretty common, Mo," Howdy said. "Aren't you used to them by now?"

Virginia said, "It's not a bad idea to be ever aware of the possibility of death."

"I'm going back to bed," Maureen said.

"I often ask myself," Virginia went on, "what would I do right now if God spoke to me and told me I had only an hour left? The answer is, I'd sit still right where I am."

"Then you're a dope," Lola said.

"I'd drink and smoke," Chris said.

"I'd go to a doctor," Stephanie said.

"No, it's too late for a doctor," Howdy said. "He can't save you now."

Stephanie shrugged and Chris grinned into his shirt front.

"Hey, please," Howdy said to him.

"I've missed something," Maureen said.

"Jesus loved a good joke," Virginia said.

"Why does everyone say that?" Maureen said. "The only joke I ever heard of Jesus telling was that time when Paul or somebody said he was a fisherman by trade, and Jesus said, 'I am, too. I fish for souls.' "

"A howl," Howdy said.

"Shecky Jesus," Chris said.

Violet appeared in the doorway. She wore still another clean suit of clothes, a Buddy Bear T-shirt and a pair of red jeans.

"Out!" Maureen said to her. "Stay the hell out! The conversation in here's unfit for a kid."

Violet ran away.

"Are you really going back to bed, Maureen?" Chris said. "Because I'm heading home if you're just going back to bed."

"Before anyone takes his leave," Virginia said, "I'd like to announce something. All of you know that Mr. Cleveland and I have talked about a wedding. It's now officially declared. We'll be wed on the twentieth, here, upstairs in the piano room. That's if everything goes right this month."

"How about I head home with you?" Maureen said.

"Me?" Chris said.

"Yeah, you," Maureen said.

"Good heavens," Virginia said.

24

Well, well, a cleanish car."

"Don't look in the back," Chris said.

"Aw, and your radio's broken. When did that happen?" Maureen said.

"Just today," Chris said. "There are some tapes under your seat, though. A few that aren't bad."

"These! You had these when *I* knew you." Maureen had put her head nearly to the floor and was searching with both hands.

"Dig behind the front ones," Chris said. "They're old." He pushed the sliding knobs for the heating system.

"Hey, I'm *down* here," Maureen said as the heater blowers threw odor and dust.

Violet bustled purposefully out of the garage. She broke into a run—her legs pounding and her short arms churning. At the same moment, the blue front doors opened and Lola's head showed.

"Wow!" Maureen was saying to Chris. "Every song Sam Cooke ever recorded."

"Go back!" Chris shouted. "You're not coming, Vi. Damn it, you're supposed to stay with Howdy!" Chris put the car in reverse and let it roll backward on the drive. "Goddamn Howdy's ass. He swore to me."

"Hold it, hold it," Maureen said. "Let's find out what's up."

Violet shot past them on Maureen's side, then whirled and palmed the window glass as Maureen was cranking it down.

"What, baby?" Maureen said.

"The lights went off," Violet said. "Please don't drive away."

Maureen called to Lola, "Is the electricity off?"

Lola bobbed her chin, stepped onto the porch, and stood arms akimbo.

"What a drag," Maureen said. She patted Violet's hand. "I believed you. Well," she said to Chris, "that's it. There's no point in me going to your hotel. Not in sheer blackness."

"It's still afternoon," Chris said. "It won't be dark for five hours."

Maureen was nodding drunkenly at Violet. "What's really the matter?" she was asking.

Chris exhaled impatience.

"Grandpa yelled at us," Violet said. "Because the air conditioner went off."

"He yelled?" Maureen said. "God! As if it was *your* fault."

"There," Chris said. The electricity had come back on, and the half-dozen porch lights that had been kept working for the storm brightened in an arch over Lola.

"Now we got it," Lola called, pointing up at the lights.

Virginia and Howdy, looking out from under the window shades, waved and gestured.

"Violet," Maureen said, "how about settling down now, okay, hon? You can go back in, watch some programs, and read the funnies. You can be with Uncle Howdy and Steph and do something they're doing."

"Couldn't I get in with you and Dad for a minute?" Violet said. "And get warm?"

"I hate to say this," Chris said, "but I'm running out of gas."

"All right," Maureen said. "Listen, Vi, you just have to train yourself to ignore your grandpa. Refuse to hear what he says, okay? You want to snooze on my bed? You can play around with the stuff in my room, and set your hair on my hot curlers."

"Yeah!" Violet said, and she charged back up the drive.

Chris let go of the brakes and drove off in reverse.

"Now let's just think a second," Maureen said.

"I can't," he said. "I'm nearly on empty." He twisted in his seat to sight where he was driving. He backed clear of the entrance gates and careened down Charity Way. "Those tools back there were the first big purchase I made with my lottery dough. They're really good."

"Up until a day ago," Maureen said, "you were a missing person who didn't give a damn about Violet or me. You weren't a bit interested."

"Yes, I was. I was interested."

"I was going to say, that you weren't concerned about me or whatever I was enduring—good or bad. I could have gotten married and had two and a half more kids."

Chris said, "I called you a hundred thousand times. In fact, if anybody ever wants to find out what happened to my fortune, that's what—I plugged it into pay phones."

"Yes? Why pay phones, Chris? I've always meant to ask. You mysteriously never called when—for however long it was—you were a guest of Quebec. And when you called from Montreal, you were usually in a phone booth in a restaurant. Maybe you didn't count on me hearing the racket in the background. Anyway, you never called from where you were living. I wonder what that was about. Big riddle." She had selected one of the cassettes. She shoved it into the tape deck. Over the music, Maureen said, "I have no idea why I suggested leaving the house with you. I think because of Howdy. But I don't know why because of Howdy. This is pointless."

"All I know is I'm running out of gas," Chris said.

"Then get some or turn off the engine!"

25

The road was striped with reflections. Deep puddles stood on the asphalt. Chris boomed through the puddles and each time the noisy, soft collision of car with water startled Maureen. They moved beside a swelling river.

"Why did you come back here, I wonder," she said.

"I wonder, too."

"Like this was home base or something. Like it's the safe tree in running bases."

"Just a place," Chris said. "And here's something I'll tell you. When you go away from here, the place disappears. Whoosh. Gone."

"This town ought to be named Ground Zero," she said. "Every few steps, something blows up in your face."

"It's not that interesting a town. You're just a fish fascinated by the bowl. No one cares about this town. Only you."

"It's my town."

The river out the window twinkled white in the premature twilight. The water got wider and turned into a reservoir backed up by a cement dam, which they drove across. They came to a village of shops. Maureen gasped. In the central parking court, blue emergency lights whipped the air from the tops of fire trucks and police cars. The front of a Burger Villa had been caved in by a felled tree. The sign for the Highlander Cleaners was splintered and knocked down. The Waffle Palace had lost all the plate glass on one side. The roof of a fabric shop lay in sections across the parking lot. Rubber trash cans were scattered around.

"Hot dog," Chris said. "They really took it on the chin here."

"I feel sorry for the waffle-place guy," Maureen said.

Chris found a wine store still open among this and that

destroyed edifice. He came out of the store hugging two cartons of Canadian ale and a sack of Cheez Doodles.

"I shouldn't eat this filth," Maureen said. "It's no better than packing material. It's a chemical invention, really. Not food in any sense of the word."

"Actually, they're good," Chris said.

Maureen munched on the Cheez Doodles and used the buckle of her loose seat belt to pry off the cap on a bottle of ale. At a stoplight, Chris thumbed orange salt from the corners of her mouth. Maureen said, "Don't overdo the gallantry, Chris. I see right through you."

"You're trying to act hard," he said. "I quit that, and I feel a lot better. Getting angry is easy. Everyone ought to fight to be softer instead. That's the test of a real person."

"Knock it off," Maureen said. "You just want me to act soft, so you can get me into bed, which is not—believe me—on the agenda."

Chris said, "I want to, of course. Sure. I'm not ashamed of it and I'm not being sneaky. But that isn't the reason I'm being nice. I'm lonely. But I'll never—I decided in Quebec—force anyone to do anything."

He accelerated, shot around a Pinto, passed a city bus on the wrong side, and flew below a traffic light that was going from yellow to red.

"Please. You know I can't stand speeding. If you don't let me out right now, I'm going to jump. I'm not kidding." Maureen popped open her door. The car slammed into a deep, black pool of water that had been hidden in the shadows under the railroad bridge. Cold water exploded into the car and blasted the windshield. She pulled her door shut. The car slowed as if stunned, and quit running. A horn went off behind them.

"My new dress," she whimpered. The cloth was streaked with stains and pasted to her. Water had gone into her nose and mouth and splashed her hair. "Fucking Ground Zero."

"Shut up," Chris said. He struggled with the ignition.

They sat in fender-high, swarming water. The engine finally started. He sped to fifty and then seventy. "Got to dry the engine with air," he said. "Brakes don't work."

"What? I want out, goddamn it!"

"Just hold it. I'm drying them."

He drove for a while with one foot on the gas, the other lightly on the brake pedal.

"I remember now," Maureen said. "I remember how it was with you." Her bottle of ale was rocking on its side on the floor mat. Creamy bubbles foamed from the bottle and mixed with the rain pooled around her shoes. "This is just about right. About the average for a day with you. Except I don't have a broken tooth yet, and we don't owe anybody a whole lot of money. Nobody's coming to evict us, so I won't have to go to a phone booth, after I bum a dime, and call my dad and ask to borrow money."

"Who was it who opened the idiot car door to jump out?"

"You are going to buy me a new dress," Maureen said. "And new shoes."

"I'll do it."

"I mean it. You're buying them and you're going to do it right now. I'm freezing, and I'll get sick otherwise."

"Consider it done," Chris said.

26

The store's phony Victorian sofa was teal blue silk, with cherry arms and legs that ended in claw feet. Chris perched there, sipped the free coffee from a delicate cup, and watched the salesgirls. They wore sweaters and heavy makeup and pants that were tight over their bottoms. One girl, in a rosy leotard, rested her weight on the cash-register counter, her back to the room. Chris was studying her spine when she twirled, throwing clean hair.

"Here we go," someone said, and Chris peeked around as Maureen came out of the dressing booth.

"Oh, hey," he said. She had on a linen frock with an indefinite, scalloped hem and a modest sunback.

"It's not what I wear," she said. She stood on her toes before a wall mirror.

"But you're wearing it," Chris said.

"It's lovely," the salesgirl said.

"You can say that again," Chris said.

"It's—you know—too cutesy for me," Maureen said.

"Yeah, a little," Chris said.

"I know what," the salesgirl said. She went and got a high-heeled shoe and a nylon stocking. She dropped to one knee and took Maureen's foot in her hands.

Chris got up from the sofa and paced around. He stood before an underwear display by the counter. The display had a cardboard cutout with a photo of a teenager. Her hands were on her hips and she was poking her tongue out. She wore candy-striped underpants. Over her tousled hair was written *Get Sassy! Get Sassy's Panties and Briefs.* Chris shook his hands and arms like an athlete preparing to heft a barbell. He glanced down the hall to the dressing booths. In a bright side stall, a muscular girl was pushing her legs into black boots. Chris looked away. He saw the salesgirl yawning and stretching, her sweater rising up her bare midriff. He crossed the store to her.

"Pardon me," she said, and covered her mouth, though the yawn had been completed. She blinked pleasantly. She had coppery red hair, china-blue eyes.

Chris said, "You know, this is a very sexy place."

"Not to me," the girl said. "Do you need help, sir?"

"Waiting for my wife," he said, stabbing a thumb in Maureen's direction. "Honestly, think about it. You've got a whispery French girl on the loudspeaker."

The redhead gave Chris—his faded shirt and dungarees and cracked leather sandals—the once-over.

"I'm just killing time," he said. "I'm not dangerous."

"Of course, sir," the salesgirl said.

"Women don't notice," Chris said. "That's what's so weird about it. You hear that music?"

"Not really. Not anymore," the girl said.

Chris said, "Doesn't it sound like a person being intimate?"

"Maybe. I guess so," the redhead said. "Granted."

"Okay. Look at all the pictures around. On that tray of underwear—the Sassy girl. Or that picture behind you." There was a poster behind the redhead, a model in a shimmery slip. "Or all the girls in the magazines you've got out on tables."

"I didn't put them out," she said.

"Of course not," Chris said. "But what if you went in a men's store, and there were blowups on the wall of guys in tiny clothes, and in magazines spread all over, and a guy on the Muzak sighing away?"

"Carol?" the redhead said. She called over her shoulder to another employee. "Tell all this to Carol."

Chris did. But then he noticed the two girls exchanging looks. "I was just killing time," he said.

"And what's your conclusion, sir?" Carol said. She was an Oriental, flawless skin, thick legs.

"Well, I don't know," Chris said. "I don't know what to make of it. I suspect you want all the men to feel uncomfortable and out of place. So they'll leave the women alone to try on the clothes and buy them."

"No," Carol said. "We love to have a girl bring a guy with her. They always spend more bread that way. The guy likes to show off. He flirts with us in front of his old lady, and drops bread to show he's a big shot. A chick alone will hassle you and give you a hard time. She'll talk herself out of clothes. But if the dude says, 'Oh, wow, that looks really groovy,' even if he's just being nice for our benefit, the chick'll always believe him and buy. My best sales are to dudes, really, not chicks. And you know something? It's not rich chicks who buy. They already know what they look good in and what they want. They can mail-order it all from New York. It's the poor chicks who'll buy anything flashy just because it looks new."

Chris said, "I once worked in a parking lot in Montreal and every day, practically every day, our rates went up another nickel. I kept noticing that it was the poor people with the carloads of kids that never complained. Never a peep out of them. It was the rich guys in their Mercedes that raised holy hell. A lot of times they'd refuse to pay at all."

The redhead smiled. She said, "Carol knows about this. At Christmas, if you get a poor enough girl from the hills and her old man in here, and you get her to try on anything at all, you've got a sale. The guy buys out of guilt at that time of year. They buy just because they're grateful you let them in the store to touch the stuff. See, they're used to discount joints where there are, essentially, no sales personnel. But here they buy crap that looks terrible and is in the wrong size and doesn't fit. And the thing is they'll never wear it."

"Fat people," Carol said. "Fat guys with fat chicks."

"Chris?" Maureen called. "What do you think?" She had traded the linen dress for a pink one with spaghetti straps.

"Yeah," he said. "Nice." He turned back to Carol. "What about fat people?"

"Ooh, look. Robin doesn't like us talking," said the redhead. She returned the glare of the salesgirl who was helping Maureen.

"She named Robin?" Chris said.

"Yes, that's Robin," Carol said. "She thinks we're blowing her sale. You're supposed to be over there, man, looking at Robin's tits."

The redhead started laughing.

"An in-joke," Carol said. "Just an in-joke. Robin is our favorite chick. She sells to the man, see? And she goes all out."

"Sell those shoes," laughed the redhead. "Sell those coats. She's half-owner. She's our boss."

"Okay," Chris said. "I promise I'll go over and look at Robin's tits if you'll tell me about fat people."

"Hey, Chris! This one or the other?" Maureen called. "Or this?" She held up a dress on a hanger.

"Let's see that one on you," Chris said.

27

Maureen was crazy about her new shoes. She put them on her hands, and danced them on the dashboard. They were oxblood leather slings with tiny gold buckles on the straps. "And this dress!" she said. She had chosen the pink one and a striped grosgrain ribbon for a belt.

"Pricey, though," Chris said as he steered and smoked.

"The one you ruined was plenty more," Maureen said.

"*I* ruined?"

"Forget it," Maureen said.

"I talked to these two girls," Chris said.

"I saw," Maureen said. "The one waiting on me said the two you were yapping with are going to get fired."

"Yours was Robin—the one waiting on you. She half-owns the store. The two I was talking to thought you should be a model. They couldn't figure out why you were with a jerky-looking guy like me."

Maureen, with effort, let out a little burp. "You're buttering me up," she said.

"No, I'm really not, Maureen."

"Oh, you sham. You farce. You ridiculous fraud."

"Hey, look," Chris said. "Can't you take an honest compliment?"

"Not when it comes from you."

"There's my place," Chris said.

Chris' motel, the Tavern Inn, was a trapezoidal building on concrete legs. It stood off a thoroughfare at the edge of the campus. The street was a fairly long drag with all-night food stores, three movie theaters, and college hangouts. The wet sidewalks were empty and smeared with reflections of pink and green. Chris swerved into the parking lot.

In the lobby, the members of a delegation of Africans sat on their luggage or stood in circles, chuckling. Flashcubes were fired. West of the lobby was a big tavern. Chris led Maureen inside. There was a circular bar in the center and lots of vinyl-upholstered booths. A huge chandelier hung over the bar and three yellow spotlights blazed from the ceiling. Otherwise, the place was dark. On a dais in the back, a trio of musicians slushed through "I Can't Get Started."

"Did I ever show you my blue-racer trick?" he asked Maureen.

"No, I don't think so."

Chris plucked a match from the book on their table and struck fire. He touched the head of the match to his whiskey and a blue flame spurted over the shot glass. He drank the flame and the whiskey.

"Blue racer," he said.

"Yeah, you did show me," Maureen said. "Very mature."

The lights in the tavern went out and came back on. The crowd of a dozen or so people moaned. Then the lights went out for good.

28

This whole wing's out," said the kid in a red tunic with brass buttons as he led them with a flashlight to Chris's third-floor room. They followed the boy out of a stairwell and down a carpeted corridor. Room doors on both sides stood open. There were low voices. People stepped into the hall behind them. The boy in the tunic stopped by a door. He shined the flashlight up on his own face, holding it like a microphone. He had pitted skin and dirty hair parted low over his eyebrows and tucked behind his ears. He was so ugly in the bizarre light that Maureen couldn't focus on what he was saying. She stared at him shamelessly, her mouth open. She twisted away when he put the beam on her and then on Chris to say good night.

"What a revolting person," Chris whispered. He turned his key in the lock.

He went immediately to the portable refrigerator on the floor by the far wall. He shoved some packaged food around, then, standing inside the refrigerator's little door, took time downing a canful of Schlitz. "Warm already," he said and belched. "Now." He got onto his knees and rolled four candles off the refrigerator's bottom shelf. Maureen leaned against the bureau and watched him light them.

They followed the candlelight into a second room. Across the room was a king-sized bed, which the maids had fixed into an orange-wrapped package. There was a divan where Chris stretched out. He kicked off his sandals.

"You have the contingency conveniences," Maureen said.

"All of them," Chris said. "That's because I've been staying in hotels so long. I even have a special showerhead I put in if I'm going to stay for like a month. Love me?"

She said, "You think it would hurt me to take two Librium after all the Scotch I had?"

"I don't know. Why do you want to?"

"No reason." She rummaged around in her bucket bag and came up with an amber bottle. She uncapped it, then slid out a couple of turquoise and black capsules. She swallowed them dry.

In the night, after the pills took effect, she lay by Chris on the bed and babbled in a throaty voice. "If the bus'd break down," she said, "we kids'd have to *walk* up that hill. Once we got snowed in. I remember Dad, for some reason, made a big kettle of lentil soup. Mom'd always fall asleep watching the TV, wake up middle of the night and yank off her socks or sweater, whatever. She never got a real night's rest. And TVs didn't last long. She burned them out. We had a dog she tied to the chaise by its leash. Pietro was its name. Mom drank big, clear cups of—smelled like pine needles—gin. Then take hot baths and lie on the—stare up at the ceiling. I remember she, her family, had a trophy company. It seemed like I went there once. I helped do something like put 'winner' on the trophies. I don't know. Mom'd sing, 'You're a weird.' No. 'You're a queer one, Julie Jordan.' I can't ever think of that song without seeing her."

Maureen went in and reluctantly out of a wheat-colored dream, her face against a foam-rubber pillow. She said, "I hear the ice-crusher machine."

"Possibly," Chris said.

"Then we have electricity. Have I been talking long?"

Three

1

Chris steered his car up the Cleveland drive. Between gear changes, he touched a light scar on Maureen's tawny knee.

"Good," he said. "Your old man's up."

"Why good?" Maureen said. "The last time he saw you, he was breaking a blood vessel to get you in jail."

"I'll square it with him," Chris said.

Cleveland was in the yard with Jack, the gardener. Both men were attached to pieces of lawn-grooming equipment. They faced each other, huddling over some joke. Cleveland was chuckling when he looked around Jack and spotted the car.

Chris braked within shouting distance. "Truce, Mr. C.? Mo and I have patched things up!"

"With used bandages!" Maureen said.

Cleveland spoke something to his gardener and they both laughed again, both looking down and away from the car.

"You get any storm damage?" Chris called.

Cleveland let his spade fall and sauntered over.

Chris said, "We saw a Waffle Palace that was blown in and lightning got a Burger Villa, it looked like. You?"

"Not too bad," Cleveland said. "A midget golf course of mine had its features rearranged. That's the only damage I've heard about." He looked to Jack for confirmation. Jack rocked his thin head yes. "We got limbs down, of course," Cleveland said.

"That's not bad," Chris said.

The gardener came part of the way to the car. He squatted on his ankles and brushed a tiny area of wet grass with his hand.

"Jack, you trying to dry out the lawn manually?" Cleveland called. "That's Jack, my yard maintenance engineer," Cleveland said to Chris.

"Stephanie's pa," Maureen said.

"Ah, Stephanie," Chris said.

Cleveland said, "So how is it?"

Maureen made a vague noise.

"You're having an anxiety seizure and can't talk?" Cleveland said.

"I'm grooving," Maureen said.

"Howdy's not grooving," Cleveland said. "His play debut —or whatever it is—is tonight. He's nervous. Lola says we all ought to be there, and she's spreading tickets around. She even dropped one on Jack."

"Seeding the audience," Chris said.

"Making an audience in the first place," Cleveland said. "The dirty weather hurt sales or something. They're afraid of an empty house."

"I'll be there," Chris said.

"Jack's going if he wants to hold this job. Aren't you, Jack?" Cleveland called.

"Maybe I'll go bull with Howdy," Chris said. "Try to calm him down. If I can do anything to help you two out, let me know."

"Usual Saturday stuff," Cleveland said. "You borrow some work clothes from Howdy. I'll give you work if you want work."

"I didn't mean for pay," Chris said.

"Neither did I," Cleveland said.

Chris reversed the car, swung it around, and followed the driveway on down the corridor that led through the poplar trees to the carriage house.

He and Maureen went up the stairway and through Howdy's open door. Howdy was studying a fat mimeographed script.

" 'The sails pant, the sea chafes, the clouds call us away!' " Howdy said. He wore black clothes and glasses with tortoise-shell frames.

"Save that throat for tonight," Chris said.

"Yeah, don't waste it on us now," Maureen said. "Wait for tonight."

Howdy smiled proudly. He looked from Maureen to Chris and back again. "How nice. How nice that you're coming, and how nice that you'll be there together."

"Are these your costume clothes?" Maureen asked.

"Naw. Just black for luck."

Maureen paged through a *Film* magazine while Howdy took Chris on a tour. Violet clambered up the steps and snubbed her mother on the way to Howdy's kitchen. Violet came out with a banana. She stood away from Maureen, gobbled some of the fruit, then dropped the rest on the floor.

"Being rude?" Maureen said. She went for the banana. Violet covered one spear of peeling with her shoe. Maureen moved the small foot. "What's your problem? Speak up."

"Leave me alone," Violet said.

"Fine, but how can I if you drop bananas on the floor instead of saying what's eating you?"

"Nothing," Violet said.

"I'm sorry you're mad."

"You left me. You and Dad went somewhere," Violet said.

Howdy and Chris came from the bedroom. There was a knocking noise from the wall next to the front door.

"That's more people wanting a tour, Howdy," Chris said. He picked up Violet and smoothed her hair.

Howdy went to the foyer and came back with a very short,

very balding black man in a suit of biscuit linen and a madras plaid bow tie.

"Lola's in the main house. The other house. She lives there actually," Howdy was saying.

The black man said, "Umm, yes, yes. Well, how stupid can I be? I recall she's mentioned her arrangements." His voice was mellifluous, his pronunciation vaguely British. He carried a big leather briefcase.

"Are you her Professor Riley? She loves your class," Maureen said.

"Lola walks in her sleep," Violet said. "Are you her dad?"

"In a way, perhaps I am," Professor Riley said. He gestured to Maureen with a cupped hand. "Don't chide her, Mother, for what she sees in the world or for what she says. She will penetrate mysteries for you if you let her. So I'm in the wrong house. As usual," the professor said.

"I love his tie, Mom," Violet said.

"All the same," Professor Riley said as he backed away. "I enjoyed bungling into all of you, and my tie thanks you, little baby child, for the compliment."

"You're welcome," Violet said.

"Smooth," Maureen said when the professor had gone.

"Butter wouldn't melt in his mouth," Chris said.

Violet said, "Why not?"

"Because he's so cool and smooth," Maureen said.

Howdy said, "One more sketch I did, Chris, I'll show you. Then I'll let you be."

"I'm okay, Howard. Show me all you want. But aren't you giving up painting?"

"I am," Howdy said. "I'm all through with painting, and rock-and-roll too, and after tonight I'm also through with theater. I'm ready to quit everything and start living."

Violet went back to the kitchen. Chris settled beside Maureen on the big couch, and waited for Howdy to bring out the last piece of art.

"I'm going to start living, too," Maureen said.

"How, specifically, do you do that?" Chris said.

"We go see our mother. That comes first," Maureen said.

Chris tilted his head to get a better biting angle on a cuticle. "Howdy," he said, "you got any beat-up clothes I could borrow? Your old man needs me for some yardwork."

"Does Chicago have Polacks?" Maureen said.

2

I can't sleep, Mom," Violet said.

They were lying under the top sheet on Maureen's bed.

"Sure you can, Violet. You're very tired." Mother and daughter twisted about and lay facing north. They turned together again and faced south.

"Feel anything?" Maureen said.

"From that pill? No. Nothing."

"Well, you will," Maureen said. "Librium always keeps its promise. And I promise you it promises to calm that tummy of yours down."

"It never wasn't," Violet said.

"Look," Maureen said. "I have to sleep some before tonight. You can't be loose while I do. So make your brain stop whirring and think of waves of water."

Violet said after a time, "A fish jumped out of my water."

Maureen was silent. Violet sat up. "Mom? What's a fox?"

"A clever little dog with red fur."

"Not a *dog,*" Violet said. "Some boys at the recreation center said *I* was a fox."

"That's nice, Vi. They were praising you. You're the dog all the other dogs chase, they were saying. The fox."

"All right," Violet said. "Now what does this mean?" She made a circle with her thumb and forefinger, then poked another finger through.

"Do you want me to tell you?" Maureen said. "You're sure?"

Violet sighed. "It's okay whatever it is."

"It all starts when you get older," Maureen said. She turned onto her back.

They looked at the ceiling while Maureen spoke. "That's when all the chemicals you have inside you begin changing you and you get bosoms. Boys, they get hairy."

"Yeck!" Violet said.

"And their complexions get oily."

"Yeck!" she said again.

"Yeah, I know," Maureen said.

"Maureen?" Lola said, from out in the hallway. "Are you dressed? There's someone with me."

"Sort of. Enough," Maureen said.

Lola and Professor Riley came in together. "Hang me," Professor Riley said. "You didn't say you were resting, you two. Let us go, Turtlidge."

"It's all right," Maureen said.

Violet was giggling. She burrowed under the sheet to the bottom of the bed, and froze.

"Dr. Riley is interested in the house, and he wanted to say good-bye to Violet," Lola said.

"If the child were here," Professor Riley said, "I'd ask her advice about something. An octogenarian friend is having a birthday and I want my gift for him to be very special. Children conceive of the most inventive ideas for gifts."

"I wish Violet was here," Maureen said.

"Your old friend will wind up with a peanut-butter bar if you listen to Violet, but that's your business," Lola said.

The form under the sheet flattened and then spurted up again. Violet surfaced next to her mother and jammed her hot face against Maureen's. "Bosoms!" she hissed into Maureen's ear. Maureen nodded yes. "Eee-yeck!" Violet said. She tried to keep eye contact with Maureen.

"Come on, Vi," Maureen said.

"Now, Violet, if you were my friend of eighty-four years of age, what would please you as a gift?" Professor Riley asked.

"Don't know," Violet said.

"I'd like to show you the attic," Lola said to Professor Riley.

"Well, I won't exploit her further," he said. "Lovely home. Lovely child. Perhaps a future president?"

"I'm sure of it," Maureen said.

"I wouldn't wish it on either of you," Professor Riley said, and made his hearty laugh.

Violet whirled on the bed to study him. She scooted sideways and covered Maureen's ear with a small hand and whispered behind the hand.

"Secrets are the salt and pepper of life," Lola said, and then looked surprised at her own words.

3

Now I really hurt," Cleveland said. It was afternoon. He and Chris were deep in the north yard by a strawberry patch just above the ravine. The door of the toolshed hung open. Three or four green and yellow enameled pieces of yard equipment stood around in the grass. Cleveland wore a headband. His bare chest was burning. His field shirt was looped by the sleeves around his waist. Chris was shirtless and in a pair of Howdy's trousers. Jack, the gardener, had gone home.

"We're about through, aren't we?" Chris said. "What's left to do but round up a few rocks?"

"They have to be the right-size rocks," Cleveland said. "I don't want any quick job done. I'll handle the carrying if you want to go lie down and have a nap."

Chris said, "I was just noticing your skin has a funny look."

Cleveland fanned a horsefly away and, with the help of his arm, sat down on the grass. "You going to borrow clothes from Howdy? For this evening?"

"I guess," Chris said. "I can't make it to the hotel and back in time to change."

"Hell, no," Cleveland said. After a time, he said, "Sunburn I don't worry about. I can shed skin. It's the inside stuff that scares me, the vital organ damage."

"You're probably fine," Chris said. "Probably healthier than I am."

"You sick?" Cleveland said.

4

And so the night began in the old house where the little girl lived and all the people went to sleep—everyone except the little girl. She said, 'It's time for me to taste the delights of this big old house.' She scrambled out of her high bed and tiptoed over to her door and first she looked to one side—"

"And then she looked to the other side. Dad? Can I tell you something?"

"I guess."

"Lola got up in the middle of the night like a zombie."

"So anyway," Chris said, "this is what the little girl did. First she looked to one side and then she looked to the other side and then she headed into the big, black hallway."

"Dad, I'm sorry."

"It's all right. What?"

"I know this story so many times."

"How could you? I made it up and I've been away for a long, long while. Who's been telling it to you?"

"I have," Maureen said. "The first part I borrowed from

you. But I always changed what the little girl did when she went downstairs."

"There's always Mr. Bullet Head," Violet said. "He chases the little girl down into the cellar with a scissors."

"Shears," said Maureen.

"With those. He chases her, going chop, chop, and cuts off her ponytail, but she gets away. And Dad?"

"Yeah?"

"I have to go to the store tonight," Violet said. "For a Chinese jump rope. Mine broke."

"Not tonight, you don't," Maureen said. "Can't you see we're dressed up and just about to leave? Sometimes, Violet, I swear!"

"You have to stay here in bed, Violet," Chris said. "That's your job."

"It's too hard to do," Violet said.

"Won't be that hard," Maureen whispered to Chris. "I've given her ten milligrams of Librium so far."

"Oh," he said, "a dopey baby."

"What'd you give me again?"

Maureen said, "Medicine. I gave you medicine to fight germs and help you sleep."

Chris and Maureen left Violet's bedroom. Her baby-sitter was downstairs in Cleveland's office—a comfortable room with a zinc and slate wet bar, leather furniture, oil paintings, a bed-sized walnut desk. On the desk were an adding machine, a typewriter, paperweights, a brass pen-and-pencil holder, and the puzzle book that the baby-sitter was filling in with neat printing. She looked up at them through wire-framed glasses.

"We're off," Chris said.

"Have a nice play," the girl said. "You know a word that starts with O and means 'unique'?"

"How many letters?" Maureen said.

"Not that kind of puzzle. I don't know," the baby-sitter said.

"How about *only*?" Chris said.

"No, it's not *only*," the girl said. "What's a film actress called Dolores blank?"

"There's Dolores Hart, Dolores Del Rio, Dolores Costello," Chris said.

"Who was the second one? Did it have an R?"

"Yeah. Two words." He spelled the name for her.

The girl bit the tip of her tongue and moved a roller-ball pen across the puzzle book.

"How about a star dog?" she said.

"Rin Tin Tin," Chris said as Maureen led him away.

"Asta. Lassie," Maureen said, dragging him.

"Benji!" the baby-sitter said.

"Who the hell is Benji? What the hell kind of a name is that for a dog star? Is this dog from Faulkner?" Chris said as they headed out of the room and into the kitchen.

"You're drunk," Maureen said.

"Impossible. No one's given me anything to drink. Here's a Breathalyzer." He kissed her mouth. "I'm happy," he said.

5

The lobby had a marble floor and plaster columns set into the walls. The air was warm and drifty with the mixed-up fruity smells of hairspray, chewing gum, and cologne. Perspiring ushers in white shirts bustled around. Girls with straight hair and long gowns took tickets at the one open door in a wall of four doors. They handed out single-sheet, folded programs. The theater was small, a three-hundred–seater painted three shades of gray.

"I feel like I'm inside a skull," Chris said, stripping off his jacket.

They all moved into their row.

"You watch," Chris said, leaning forward to speak to the lineup of Maureen, Lola, Stephanie, Virginia, and Cleveland. They all leaned forward and listened to Chris. "You watch. How long does it take you to read this whole program? To memorize it, practically? Two minutes? But the crowd here will spend the entire evening studying the thing like it's the Magna Carta."

Maureen glanced around. The theater was three-quarters full, and everyone who was not talking or hunting a seat had his nose in a program.

"I'm so nervous," Stephanie said. She and Lola and Virginia were exchanging hand pats.

Maureen was hungry for a cigarette. She longed for the curtain to rise.

"Where's Howdy?" Cleveland said. He was searching the handout for Howdy's name. "Almost everyone listed is a girl."

"On the back," Lola said.

"Production assistant?" Cleveland said. "Is that all?"

"Shhh, Dad," Maureen said. "I can hear you way over here."

"The evening's in three parts," Lola explained. "Howdy hasn't anything to do with the first two parts. But he's in the cast of the last part, after the intermission. See? And he helped with the set design, I guess. And he assisted with the production. Three listings for his name, like Orson Welles or something."

"Hell, I thought he wrote the whole shebang and was the star," Cleveland said.

"Shhh," Lola said. "Quit now."

Maureen was watching an usher who was joking with a white-haired man and calling him "Dr. Bob."

"Hey, Chris," she said. "Chris!" He was reading his program.

"Yeah?"

"See that guy? Hurry up and look. He's going up the aisle. Not the usher in blue. The one with the glasses."

Chris had to twist and partly stand to see. "Okay, I saw him," he said.

"He's an asshole," Maureen said.

"Speaking of which—" Chris nodded at the huge man who had just taken the seat directly in front of him. The man had oiled, wavy hair and enormous shoulders. "The biggest head in the world," Chris said. The man's wife turned sharply and grinned at Chris. She turned back. Chris hooked his fingers in his mouth, stretched his lips, popped his eyes, and waggled his tongue at her head. The huge man caught Chris doing it. "Please don't eat me," Chris said.

Maureen smiled.

"Leaky barge. Pious gob of slobber," Chris said very softly.

Maureen turned to Chris. "Vomit," she said.

"Rat vomit?" Chris said.

Lola leaned forward. "Babies!" she said with disgust. "Eight-year-olds! Worse than Violet. Far worse."

"Here we go," Maureen said.

The houselights died. The curtain rose. From the ceiling, from speakers that looked like flying saucers, came an amplified prelude to a Bach suite for unaccompanied viola. The music was busy, lonely, linear.

Downstage center, a girl in a raspberry tutu and tights posed in a difficult arch. White light shone from both wings. The girl began dancing in place—curling, bending, sticking out one leg or the other. "There's rat vomit now," Chris said.

"Yeah, that's her," Maureen said.

"Big idiots," Lola said. "She's good. What she's doing is hard."

The music faded and was replaced by random bursts of percussion. But the switch had no effect on the slowly unwinding dancer. A tub was thumped. Cymbals shivered. The dancer's elbow jutted. She lifted a knee, curled her toes.

Heavier girls in leotards zoomed out from the wings. "Buffalo vomit," Maureen said. The girls jumped and spun in unison. Their feet made patting noises and skid sounds on the stage.

Chris said, "They've come to test the strength of wood."

Lola batted Maureen's head as she sometimes did Violet's.

"What'd *I* do?" Maureen said.

The music changed to bluegrass banjo, then abruptly stopped. The girls danced in silence. The one in the tutu crashed to a halt, turned to the audience, and spoke for several minutes in a low singsong. All Maureen could get were some mentions of various constellations and a U.S. secretary of defense.

The second part of the entertainment was better. There were flats and scrims on the stage, props and furniture to look at, and actual actors. Maureen thought one of them was cute—a boy in too much mascara. She watched him almost exclusively. Chris had fallen asleep, so Maureen said to Lola, "Look at the guy in the corner."

"Isn't he darling?" Lola said.

At intermission, they all went out to the lobby, and Chris, stretching and rubbing his eyes, gave his review of the first two playlets. "I toss my hat in the air in excitement for, and in appreciation of, these two samples of regional theater. They inspire us to dream. In my many years of theatergoing, I don't recall a production so irresistibly inspiring."

"Not funny," Lola said.

Maureen said, "I never thought I would be, but I'm coming apart with nerves for poor Howdy. Dad is, too. You can tell."

"From the very instant the curtain went up, one felt himself lifted from himself," Chris said.

"Be quiet," Maureen said.

"You know, that was enjoyable," Cleveland said. "Very professional."

"I'm not sure I understood it all," Virginia said. "But it was impressive and very stimulating."

"Inspiring," Chris said.

"I'm nervous for Howdy," Lola said. "But what's the worst that could happen?"

"Just wait," Chris said.

Howdy's play had a musical overture described in the program as a "work for electronic strings and percussion." When a rock ballad played over the loudspeakers, the crowd kept circulating and having intermission. The houselights blinked repeatedly. "It's time," Maureen said.

She dragged the party back to their seats.

Chris said, "I thought someone was just snapping the lights to the music. Where's our giant? If he doesn't sit in front of me, I'll be forced to look at the stage."

The curtain ascended a little way, stopped, started up again, stopped, dropped back down.

"Howdy's handling the curtain," Chris said.

People in the dark theater were battling for their seats, climbing over shoes and ankles. A needle scraped the amplified recording. The rock ballad began again.

"Howdy's in charge of the music too," Chris said.

Lola swatted Maureen and shook a finger at Chris. "I'm warning you," she said.

The big man and his wife fumbled down their row, making a lot of noise, apologizing. They fell, more or less, into their seats.

"Good," Chris said. "Total eclipse."

The rock ballad trailed off into silence. A change in the lighting signaled the curtain's second attempt to rise.

"What?" Lola said when the stage was exposed.

"Oh, Howdy," Maureen said. "Oh, Lord, no."

Chris craned his neck to see around the giant man. "What?" he said to Maureen.

Stephanie squealed.

On the stage, right down in front, Howdy was standing sideways. He was wearing an athletic supporter. He was making a gesture with his arms, raising them toward the ceiling. His thin body was painted with makeup so that he seemed to be not so much naked as wearing a naked suit. Over his head in a white spotlight was his painting of his family, and floating above the original line of portraits was a freshly rendered Stephanie in exact anatomic detail. Howdy had added crude, balloonlike bosoms on his sister's and mother's portraits—white circles with apple-red bull's-eyes. Lola's figure had an exposed belly swollen round as a manhole cover and painted a purplish cocoa.

Lola began talking, using her normal loud speaking voice, until Maureen pressed a hand over her mouth.

"Are you people crazy?" the giant, who had turned, said.

"Thank God," Cleveland called out. Two actresses who were playing Howdy's daughters hastened forth with a choir robe to cover their naked father, whereupon Howdy started a recitation. He spoke of the mountains and valleys of women, and of the pillars that men have. He narrowed in on the subject of incest.

Maureen, with her hand still over Lola's mouth, said, "Chris, if you don't quit laughing, you'll never see Violet again."

"My mother's loins," Howdy said in a tender, tortured voice. He pointed to the oil painting, to the picture of his mother.

"Shut up!" Cleveland yelled, and was booed and shushed by the crowd.

Chris turned his gaze away from the stage, his fingers in his ears, humming intently.

"Oh, sweet, sisterly love!" Howdy declared from the stage.

6

I've told you three times. Now, I'm telling you again, but I'm getting hoarse, so please listen! I did not write that play. It was not about you. You weren't in that play. None of you! I was acting in a play about Greek people and mythological people, that was written in nineteen twenty who-knows, and translated, and neither the author nor the translator has ever met you, so how could he write a play about you? Richard Allen, who did the sets, saw my big painting and asked me if I'd change a few things—like adding the big bosoms and making one person pregnant—so that we could use it as a drop to clarify who-was-who during my opening speech."

"Don't get near me," Maureen said. Howdy had paced to within five feet of the living room couch, where Maureen sat in her new dress.

"And what about Stephanie? Did she know you were going to hold her naked body up for everyone to look at while you paraded around without a stitch on?" Cleveland said. He drank an iced Coke.

Howdy sighed gigantically. "For the fifth time, that wasn't Steph. It was her head—they were all your heads. Steph's body was Judy Allen's, Richard Allen's wife. You met them, Chris. At the cafeteria, remember?"

Chris said, "Yeah, the one who burned her lunch." He stared into his Perrier, and kept a level, even expression. No one had liquor because Virginia had asked them to prove they could stay away from it for one night.

"Everyone thought it was Stephanie," Cleveland said.

"Not really," Virginia said.

"I was deeply embarrassed for her," Cleveland said.

"I think I looked good," Stephanie said.

"It was shit," Cleveland said. "Obscene, unpoetic shit."

"Didn't you pay attention?" Howdy said. "If you'd paid attention, you might've noticed that a big war was just over, that the family of the guy I was portraying had just been slaughtered in the big war."

"All I heard was about people having holes drilled in their ankles and being dragged around behind cars," Maureen said.

"The cars were *chariots*," Howdy said. "It was a modern version of ancient Greek warfare."

"That was me up there," Lola said.

"It wasn't exactly *you*, Lola. Good God, I'd expect this from the rest of them, but not you. You go to college. You write poetry. You've studied the Greeks and Greek tragedy. It's erotic, sure. But this playwright just de-abstracted the violence and sex. He put them into terms we can really see and hear. Listen to my voice—it's a croak! You're all grinding me down." He slumped on the hearth and seemed to lose mass before their eyes.

"I think I know the problem here," Chris said. "The problem is not that you were in the play, Howdy, but that you invited everyone to come and you didn't prepare us for it."

"I forgot that you're all a bunch of imbeciles," Howdy said. "I forgot that, yes."

The front door chimed, and Chris went to answer it. He called from the hall for Howdy and Stephanie.

Jack was standing just inside the door. He wore a suit and tie under a raincoat. He was red-eyed and swaying.

"Did you want a ride?" he said to Stephanie.

"Hello, Dad," she said.

"Didn't you want a ride?"

"Howdy's going to drive me to Aunt Pearl's for the night. Don't you remember?"

"You want a ride home?" Jack said.

"Honestly, Jack," Howdy said, "you're stoned. I'll drive you both home."

Jack threw a crisp punch into Howdy's right eye. Howdy's head snapped back, and Chris caught him by the shoulders. Jack winced, grabbing his own big knuckles.

"Rich dick-suck," Jack said.

Howdy was on him a second later, pinning him to the door. Twice, Howdy's clumsy roundhouse blows landed on wood, but most of them struck the drunken man.

Stephanie watched without much expression.

Howdy fell onto all fours and heaved for breath. Chris moved to help him. Howdy sobbed or coughed or both.

Jack got down on one knee next to Howdy. Blood dribbled from his nostrils. He was trying to talk: "I got a gun in the truck. I'll kill your ass."

Howdy threw a rubbery-armed haymaker and missed. On its way back, his open hand slapped Jack's eye and damaged nose.

Jack moaned and said, "Ouch. You dick-suck."

"Go," Howdy gasped. "Go from my house!" He raised a fist to strike again.

"This is plain crazy," Chris said, stepping between the men

Howdy reached around Chris's leg and bumped Jack's nose. Jack said, "Whoa, no," and crazily swatted the air around him as though he were after a bee. Howdy collapsed onto his side.

"All right," Cleveland said. "Let's settle down, you knotheads."

7

Cleveland was laughing and petting his dotted necktie, stroking it from knot to point. There was color on his neck, above his starched shirt collar. "Oh, damn, damn, damn, that was great. That was so great." He beamed, stroked his tie, looked contentedly around the room.

Virginia sat with her back straight. On her lap was a dish with a square of coffee cake. Her knees were pressed together.

"I'm not sorry about a thing," Howdy said from the sofa, where he lay on his back, a wrapped ice cube held to his eye. Sooty mascara tears from the melted ice streaked his face.

"Not sorry neither," Cleveland said. "My heavens, no. Old Jack thumped you a good one for that nonsense. Now none of us has to."

"That illiterate," Howdy said.

"He had the right, kiddo," Cleveland said. "You showed his daughter naked."

Chris whispered to Maureen, "Jack's my kind of drama critic." They also were on their backs, on the floor, with plates of coffee cake on their stomachs.

"And I'm not mad at you anymore," Cleveland said to Howdy. "By God, you took your medicine and you came back swinging."

"Gee, thanks," Howdy said.

"Jack's a tough rattlesnake to tangle with," Cleveland said. "Aren't you, Jack?"

Jack looked as though he had been flung with great force into the deep armchair. His big, quivering hand had the knuckles taped. He held a glass of bourbon and a Pall Mall cigarette with a two-inch stick of ash at the tip. The ledge of his brow was bumpy from blows. His stockinged feet were laid one on top of the other. His eyes were closing.

"You're okay, aren't you, Jack?" Howdy said.

"Don't you worry about it," Jack said. "It's not Saturday night without a fight."

"Howdy came running at you, didn't he, Jack?" Cleveland said.

"Didn't he just," Jack said. He moved his drink hand forward and backward in an ambiguous gesture. He lost the ash on his cigarette to the rug.

Lola licked butter from her fingers and said she'd be going to bed soon. "This has been the worst day of my life," she said.

"Before you go," Cleveland said, "Ginny and I have something we want to announce, if Chris and Maureen will stop whispering and listen."

On the floor, Chris and Maureen were laughing and having a separate conversation. "We know, Dad, we know," Maureen said. "Unless this is a new one."

"I told you," Virginia lashed out at Cleveland. "I told you, I've already announced everything. Yesterday after the tornado."

"About the marriage?" Cleveland said.

"Yes!" Virginia hissed with such heat that Cleveland's mouth dropped open. "Were you having an alcoholic blackout when I told you?"

"Hey, give her a belt," Jack said. "She's slipped her harness."

"Yeah," Chris said, and Maureen laughed. "Whomp her one in the chops, Mr. Cleveland."

Stephanie was on her backside with her legs drawn up. She looked pale, dull-eyed. "Dad, please? Please, can't we go home?"

"I wanted to tell them," Cleveland said. "I mean I wanted us both to tell them."

Maureen said, "On the twentieth, in the piano room, everyone's invited, small ceremony, reception on the lawn."

"Well, what do you think, Maureen? Howdy?" Cleveland said.

"Oh, I give up," Virginia said. "I already told you what they think. They couldn't care less. No, indifference is too mild a term for what they feel. They feel overt hostility."

"She's got it," Maureen said.

"Pay no mind," Lola said. "It sounds lovely."

"It does, indeed," Cleveland said.

"I forbid you to talk about my wedding at this time,"

Virginia said. "I'm much too aroused. You'll be glad to know, Maureen, that I am leaving here soon, so you can all hit the liquor closet and get yourselves intoxicated and have more fistfights."

"Don't think we won't," Maureen said.

"Come on, Mo," Howdy said.

"Dad, please, let's go," Stephanie said.

Howdy put a battered hand in her frizzy hair, but she jerked away.

"Soon as I finish my drink," Jack said. "But I don't know why you're in such a hurry to get home. You got my belt waiting for you when you do."

Howdy struggled to sit up. "I'll kill you if you touch her."

"Uh oh," Lola said.

Virginia began to pray. She put her hands together and closed her eyes and lifted her face to the ceiling.

"Jesus, fuck," Maureen said.

8

I swear I can smell Violet out here," Chris said. He was rocking a swing.

"It's the soap," Maureen said.

"Yeah, the soap," Chris said. "But no soap you could buy."

"Little-kid scent," Maureen said.

They went along a path that cut through a tree barrier, and then along the rock wall that lined Charity Way. There was a mild flutter of rain.

"Remember going to the golf course on this kind of night?" Chris said.

"Yeah."

"Hey, stop walking," he said. "Boy, some of those golf-course nights."

"I remember them differently probably. For me, it was just bugs and wet everything. And I was always afraid Dick VanZandt would come whizzing up on his motorized cart and put his searchlight on us."

"Dick VanZandt!" Chris said. "How the hell'd you remember his name? The security guy in his goddamn security golfmobile."

"I was always afraid he'd blast us with that searchlight and then take a flash photograph and give it to my dad. And there was always somebody moving around on those greens, too. Sitting on sprinklers or eating live chickens or God knows," Maureen said.

Chris said, "VanZandt, you may know, stepped into the propeller of a pontoon plane in Hanoi and went to rock-and-roll heaven."

"Magnificent," Maureen said. "I really wanted to hear that." They walked in silence awhile. She said, "Now I have something to tell you, and it's this. I want you to go away awhile."

"I'm not doing a thing. What am I doing?"

"Ever since you got here, things have been exploding in my face. Fights, tornadoes, floods, theatrical flops. I blame them all on you—fair or not. I don't know what blew you back from Canada. I'll never know the real, whole truth, probably, but that's okay with me. Keep your secrets." Her gaze came back to him. "Anyway, you're here now, and as usual, you're making trouble happen. I believe in my heart of hearts that you're the cause of everything. I believe it like Virginia believes in Jesus. I have faith in your power to bring chaos."

"If you want to be insane, Mo, how can I argue?" he said.

"It wouldn't matter if you did argue. I've decided. Just go away and let me regroup. I have serious things going on in my head right now. For one thing, what I'm going to say to my mother to show I forgive her."

"You want her to forgive *you*," Chris said. "You and your

dad. You must have been some unpleasant little six-year-old for her to leave and not write or phone or anything for all this time. For her to dump you and never look back."

Maureen said, "Don't come here again, Chris. Don't call me. Don't go to campus and be around Howdy. Don't ever try to see Violet. Don't send a telegram. Disappear for a while, okay?"

"How long a while?"

"A week—minimum."

"May I ask you one question?"

"No."

"Will you be gone for Ireland in a week?"

"Probably not, no. If I am, I'll let you know, so you can say good-bye to Violet."

"One week," Chris said. "You get one week, Maureen. But so help me, I'm going to pay you back for this in some way."

"That's the old Chris," Maureen said. "Threats. That's more like the prick you really are."

9

Virginia was wearing only a thin brassiere and skimpy underpants. They were expensive pieces of underwear, silk, a color the saleswoman called taupe. Virginia's body was tan and sleek, well-muscled but soft. "Like a hula dancer's," the saleswoman had said.

"You are something," Lola said.

"How nice." Virginia was weeping seriously and with great concentration.

"Most nude women I see, I want to turn away fast. Old *and* young. But you're like Violet. I don't see any faults at all. Smooth as a seal."

Virginia, crying and smiling, said, "Well, that's a delightful thing to say." She lifted her arms and turned in front of Lola.

"Perfect," Lola said.

They were upstairs, in a walk-in dressing closet that had full-length mirrors on two walls.

Virginia held up some of her hair. "This is just hay," she said, her voice rippled by a sob. Virginia used the hair as a towel, crying into it.

In the week since Howdy's play, they had had tornado watches or warnings almost every day. The temperature had been in the high nineties, the humidity insufferable. On this day, Saturday, a warm and bitter rain was falling, and the sky had turned dark enough that Lola had gone around and switched on the lamps.

Cleveland had been ugly. On Wednesday, he had complained of a toothache and washed down his breakfast omelet with Bloody Marys. He had nursed a drunk until early evening, then gone upstairs to bed, leaving Virginia with dinner guests from his upstate bottling-plant operation. On Thursday, he had stayed in his room, sick. He hadn't eaten. On Friday, he was better. He accompanied Virginia to the caterer's and to the dressmaker who'd be doing her wedding gown. He had helped her with the invitations, kept an appointment with the minister, taken her to an elegant dinner. He had downed a lot of vodka with their meal, and more vodka later in the penthouse lounge of a downtown skyscraper.

The lights, the view, the height had been exhilarating to Virginia, but Cleveland had turned sour. More than once he had patted the behind of their waitress, who was costumed as a French maid. He had snapped her garter finally, and been refused more drinks. He and Virginia were asked to leave. In his bedroom, he had tried to make sloppy, dizzy love to her, and she had answered with a dainty slap on his cheek.

"There, that does it," she had said. "I've never hit anyone in my life, and now I have. I've never been asked to leave a restaurant, and now I have. You and your family upset me.

But right now I am more disgusted than upset. I told myself I'd never marry anyone with whom I could have a quarrel, and now that's just what you and I are doing."

She put on a slim gray dress and let Lola do up the back.

"The hardest thing about being good isn't the being good," Virginia said. "It's being around people who never make a particle of effort themselves. All they do is try to knock you off course and corrupt you."

"That's true around here," Lola said. "I get so mad, it can't be good for me."

"Rage is not good for you," Virginia said. Her eyelids were swollen. "I really don't need you any more today, dear heart. The rest of what I have to do is just checking color schemes and selecting the garlanding for the room and seeing if this blue would go better with the walls than the green or the pale yellow—for the bridesmaids' dresses—and ten zillion other details."

"I'm available for details," Lola said. "Holding things up—patterns. I mean, I'm really getting excited about this wedding stuff. Being in on the ground floor and all."

Virginia answered with a mighty sob.

10

Lola mooned around in the living room. She watched the sopped lawn and driving rain from a front window. She fanned herself with a magazine, then practiced balancing the magazine on her head. She got fed up with that and rapped on Cleveland's door.

"It's open," he said in a thin voice.

She found him in his boxer shorts standing uncertainly in the center of the room. He looked frightened.

"Heart attack, I think," he said.

"You? Where? I mean, where does it hurt?"

"Heart," he said.

"Then you're probably okay," Lola said. "You can breathe all right?"

Cleveland took a test breath. "I can't tell," he said.

"How do your arms feel? Your shoulder?"

"I know what you're getting at. But Sid Golis was knocked over by his heart, down on the seventh green of the golf course, and I was there. He lived, but he told me later it felt like a crowbar blow on his heart. On his *heart.*"

Lola fetched a robe for Cleveland. He put it on, moving gingerly as an invalid. "You're just guilty about all the booze last night."

"It isn't helping," Cleveland said. "But I've had a warning from a medical man."

"So has everyone over twelve," Lola said.

"I'm dying."

"You'd get better fast if you could see what I just saw. Your bride-to-be in her undies."

"That doesn't matter now," Cleveland said. "I'm not interested." His voice was soft and strained.

"Brand new drawers. Little tiny ones," Lola said.

Cleveland grinned. "She *is* something. Her throat's sort of old, but the rest of her could pass for thirty-five. Her knees are sort of old, too."

"What's this?" Lola said, pushing fingers into Cleveland's waist. "What's all this?"

"The sauce, Lola, is what it is."

"And your hair looks lousy," she said.

"It's thinning," he admitted.

"You're lucky to get that woman, awful-looking thing like you."

She left him and got an umbrella from a stand in the foyer. She headed for Howdy's apartment.

The door on the landing was open. She climbed the steps.

She found everything in the apartment wrecked. The furniture was overturned, the pictures—except for the family portrait—lay dumped on the floor. Broken glass was all over the rug, as was dirt from thrown and tipped-over house plants. Howdy's junk sculpture was in pieces in a corner. The walls were stripped of everything except a pencil sketch of the first Mrs. Cleveland drawn from an old photograph.

She found Howdy in his jump suit on the bed.

"Can you talk about it?"

"It's Stephanie," he said.

"She cheated on you."

Howdy shot off the bed and threw himself at a wall. He sat on the floor and kicked the wall with his shoes until he had made cracks and the start of a hole. He said, "You don't care. You're glad."

"I don't care about her. But I care about you. And there's nothing I can do. Love hurts."

"Love hurts," Howdy said.

"I'd like to give you a big, sexy kiss," Lola said.

He draped an arm over her shoulder. They strolled around the apartment. Howdy stopped and flicked on a recording of Mahler's Ninth Symphony for them to walk to.

"Oh, this is good. You did that well," Lola said as they examined the damage he'd done.

"You think I did okay?" Howdy said.

Lola made instant coffee in the kitchenette. "You didn't get around to the plates and cups in here," she said. She spun a cake platter at the refrigerator. The plate bounced whole onto the floor.

"That's what happened to me too," Howdy said.

He tried to right the sofa, couldn't, and sat on its bottom. He sipped coffee. "I went to pick her up last night. Jack met me in the driveway. I smelled it right away. He took me inside the house—first time I'd ever been in—and there was this big hayseed. Jack introduced him and the guy crushed my hand, shaking it. He was Jeff. Jeff was also waiting for Steph, Jack told me."

"I get the picture," Lola said.

"When she came out, it was Jeff she went to. I love her," Howdy said.

"It gets changed for hate. Real slowly, but it will," Lola said.

"I just want to call her up and ask what she thought she was doing," Howdy said.

"Don't do that," Lola said.

"Yeah, but I think Jack made her put on that show."

"He couldn't make her," Lola said.

"You know what I thought? I thought Jeff could be her brother, and Jack had talked them into this thing for me, to pay me back for pounding him."

"That's really reaching," Lola said. "Settle down."

"I'm seriously considering giving her a call."

"Don't, Howdy," Lola said.

11

She walked in on Maureen, who was in the kitchen, dressed in a slip, talking on the wall phone.

"What's the story today?" Lola said. "Why's the whole family in their B.V.D.s? Bunch of nudists all of a sudden. You know, it's raining. You could get electrocuted."

"Hold it," Maureen said into the telephone. "Lola, do you notice I'm having a conversation with somebody?"

"Electrocute yourself," Lola said. "See if I care."

She went to her room and plopped onto her bed. She decided to call up Professor Riley, but before she could dial, she heard the telephone version of Chris's voice. She listened for a while.

He was saying, "A rocking chair in there. A pretty big, leafy backyard. There's two girls about Violet's age, and a hundred other kids—university people's kids. I think I have access to a garage."

Maureen's voice said, "Unh."

"So," Chris said. "This kitchen's not great. But they swore to me there were no roaches."

"Um," Maureen said.

"Well, I haven't seen any. And I didn't find any old boxes of Roach Away in the cupboards. It's a nice apartment, Mo, if you ever want to come here, especially since your old man's bringing that evangelist lady into the house. Here you'd have a free, safe, private, orderly place. That's before you go to Ireland or if you come back. Or you could think about moving out to start Violet in the university school down here in the fall, which I hear is a really great school. Is that you gulping, Lola? Are you on the line?"

"It's me swallowing my incredulity," Lola said.

"Hi, Lola," Maureen said.

"Hi, Maureen."

Chris said, "Well, will you just give it a look, Mo? It is a nice apartment. Maybe you really will like it. You don't know."

"What do you think, Lola?" Maureen said.

"I just want to use the phone," Lola said.

"Please," Chris said.

"He sounds safe enough," Lola said.

"I've been cleaning all week, getting ready, and I haven't called once, have I, Lola?" Chris said.

"No, he didn't call."

"So, will you come?" Chris asked her.

"To look. I'll come to look."

Lola put down the receiver and went into her wide, bright bathroom. She splashed cold water on her face. She washed her hands. She went back to the bedroom and listened on the phone for a dial tone. She dialed Professor Riley's number. His wife answered.

"Yes," Lola said.

"Yes?" Mrs. Riley said.

"Yes, this is Lola Turtlidge, one of your husband's students."

"Yes?"

"A lot of yeses," Lola said. "I need to talk to Dr. Riley some. About schoolwork."

"Right. Well, he's not here now, and he's not in his office on Saturdays. Can you tell me what it's about, Lola? So that I can tell him?"

"Are you a Negro?" Lola said. She slapped herself on the forehead. Mrs. Riley didn't answer. "I mean, in your husband's sense of the New Negro?"

"I don't understand," Mrs. Riley said.

"Me neither," Lola said. "That's why I'm calling. I'm trying to write this poetry for my portfolio and it's supposed to be informed by the consciousness of the New Negro, which is what it says here in my notes. I feel stupid. I don't know what that means, and it just occurred to me that maybe you could explain it," Lola said. "In terms I'd understand."

"Maurice has his work and I have mine, and we don't bring it home with us," Mrs. Riley said. "I have no idea what you're talking about. None at all. It's not my field."

"What's your field?" Lola said, and slapped herself again.

"I'm a doctor of veterinary medicine, and I have a peach pie bubbling over in my oven, I'm afraid."

"Oh, shit," Lola said.

"So I have to go, but I'll tell Maurice you called about your poetry problem, and then he'll decide whether to get back to you on his weekend or save it until Monday. You're a Negro?" Lola heard a smile behind the question.

"Just on weekends," Lola said.

"So you're one of my husband's girls?"

"Oh, I'm just a plain old girl," Lola said.

"All right. I think Lola is a very lovely name. I'll tell Maurice the girl with the pretty name of Lola called. Now I really must go." Mrs. Riley hung up.

Lola smiled and walked around her room. Without thinking about it, she began to tidy things up. Without tasting, she bit into a yellow apple that was on her nightstand.

In the small, formal living room, she found Cleveland, Virginia, and Violet. Cleveland was immaculately dressed in a navy suit, soft white shirt, black wing tips. His face, though, was a vivid pink, his eyes glassy, his hair mussed. He poured and drank champagne from a bottle that he kept in the crotch of his crossed legs. Virginia wore a red gingham check with nine crinolines under the skirt and a starched white apron on top. There were pigtails, tied off with red yarn, above her ears. Violet was sitting on the carpet, silent, pondering.

"Miss Virginia," Lola said.

"We're doing a taping this afternoon for the show tomorrow morning. I suppose you knew we weren't live."

"I had no idea."

"Isn't she adorable?" Cleveland said. "Did you ever think Ginny could be so adorable?"

"She's got nothing to be ashamed of," Lola said.

"That's what I'd say," Cleveland said. "Good old Miss Virginia. Quite a piece."

"I'm sure Violet is interested," Virginia warned.

"I'm sick," Violet said.

Cleveland jammed his cuff back from his wrist and scowled at his watch. "It's about time. You nervous?"

Virginia said, "Lola, I'm surprised you're still around. Don't you get away from these maniacs on your free days?"

"Nothing to do," Lola said, and shrugged heavily.

"It's a good thing you're here," Cleveland said. "Maureen took the Saab to visit Chris and left the baby here with me. You'll have to watch her for us, Lola. But if you don't complain about it, you'll get a raise starting Monday."

"Big deal," Lola said.

Cleveland finished the champagne, drinking the rest from the bottle. Virginia made an angry face at him.

"A big raise," Cleveland said. "You can thank Virginia for it."

"Double," Lola said.

"All right, I'll double it," Cleveland said. "Your salary is doubled."

"I can't take you to the studio when you're like this," Virginia said.

Cleveland said, "The old ranger is fit and he solemnly promises to be good around the kiddies."

"I can't go?" Violet said.

"For the last time, no," Cleveland said. "Your turn is later this month."

"It's policy, dear," Virginia said. "We have to be strict. Some days there were fifty children there, all belonging to station people and not one with an invitation. You understand."

"I don't," Violet said.

"She does," Lola said.

"It's unfair," Violet said.

"What isn't?" Lola said.

Cleveland was having trouble getting up from the couch.

12

Chris was breathing grandly. His bare chest, back, and shoulders were wet from the humidity. He blotted his face with a flowered towel. He wore flannel bathing trunks.

The small lobby where Maureen stood was without ornament. It was fragrant in the heat with the sweet perfume of decaying wood and the confusing aromas of past cooking.

They climbed a flight of steeply graded stairs. On the landing, Chris said, "Here's home." He opened a door on a corridor hung on both sides with shadowy old clothes. The passageway was stuffy, the air thick with moth crystals and mold. The light source was a bulb high on the ceiling of the chamber. Chris shoved aside a velveteen curtain at the end of the corridor and brought them into a very small room. There were three tall windows, and a buttoned, built-in couch. In one of the windows roared an air conditioner from Sears.

Maureen put herself on the window seat and sighed in the refrigerated air. The view was of maple branches, the side of a neighboring house, and on the ravaged brick drive stood her father's Saab. It was blocking the way of a tiny kid in bib pants who was struggling with a wheel toy.

There were full bookshelves. They held legal volumes, technical volumes, black-leather notebooks in series. In a stack on the couch were some new paperbacks, each with a neatly torn square of paper marking a page.

"Well, I like it," Maureen said.

Chris turned to the walls and studied them. He touched a crack that led from a stray nailhead. "It will be awfully nice, I think. Private for you and me and Violet. You're looking doubtful."

"That's because I feel doubtful. Let's see the rest."

The rest of Chris's apartment was an oblong room a second flight up, with a rocker, several stuffed chairs, a bed on the floor. "This is dying," Maureen said when she passed a giant avocado plant.

The dining area had a picnic table and a bench, both behind a hinged and paneled screen. Maureen inspected a framed picture on an otherwise bare wall. "Is this real?"

"It's a real oil painting, not a print," Chris said. "But it's not the original. It's a copy. The very first thing I bought with my lottery money."

"How odd," Maureen said.

13

I'm Bob Breevort," said a pear-shaped young man.

"This is Bobby," Virginia said.

"I'm very pleased to make your acquaintance, sir," Bobby Breevort said, pulling Cleveland's hand. "I believe, sir, you and I are neighbors, inasmuch as our plantations abut."

"You're the oldest Breevort kid?" Cleveland said.

"I have that privilege, sir."

"You're Ted Breevort's boy? Live up Charity Way in the brick French place? And now you work in TV?"

"He's very quick, isn't he?" Bobby Breevort said to Virginia. He gestured to a member of his crew.

Cleveland said, "Sure. I know you, sure. You came around in drag for trick-or-treat once. That's you, isn't it?"

Breevort winked at Virginia. To her, he said, "He's a treasure."

"That was the best Halloween rigout I've ever seen. This kid had me completely buffaloed," Cleveland said to Virginia.

"It's good to see you," Breevort said. He folded his arms

around a clipboard and held it to his chest. "How's the rest of the family? Howdy?"

"Howdy's your age," Cleveland said.

"Nice to know he's keeping up." Breevort touched Cleveland's arm and winked at him.

A girl in painter's pants joined them. She said, "Bobby, about half the monkeys are here. Curt's got 'em down the hall for graham crackers. Lights are almost hot enough. Curt'll do prep in another fifteen. Maybe Ginny should go into makeup."

Breevort consulted a stop watch that hung from a long string around his neck. Also around his neck were headphones. The set for Virginia's show was being assembled by two scruffy teenagers. The brightly colored flats were cracked and taped and peeling. Breevort sent the girl away. "Showtime's coming. Ginny, you want to go into makeup?"

"I'd like to see that," Cleveland said.

"Makeup," Virginia said, "is just me standing over by that mirror putting on makeup."

"I can get lost if you want," Cleveland said.

"Time for me to look busy," Breevort said.

"Where can I stand to be out of the way?" Cleveland said.

Breevort said, "Anywhere but in front of that camera. Say, do you want to go on today? Do you want to be in the show?"

"Hell, yes," Cleveland said.

"No," Virginia said.

"Well, you two hash it out," Breevort said. "I'm off to the control booth." He walked away, pushing off the balls of his feet with each step so that his gait moved him in a lively fashion. He looked to Cleveland twice Howdy's age. His sparse hair was high off his brow, his fleshy face was already seamed with wrinkles, his short body was bottom-heavy.

"That's a very special young man," Virginia said.

"Looking at him," Cleveland said, "I just realized my kids don't look near as old as they're supposed to."

Virginia sent Cleveland through heavy doors and down a

hallway. On the cinder-block walls were enlarged black-and-white photographs of local newscasters—one of Virginia. It was an old picture. She had had darker hair, twinkling eyes, painted-on freckles.

Cleveland entered a big room, a cafeteria with long benches attached to long tables. There was an assortment of grown-ups in casual Saturday clothes who sat with children in dresses and suits. Children who weren't seated were running and yelling and throwing things. A boy Violet's size was weeping. A man dressed as a clock was at the front of the room, making some kind of announcement.

"Lavatory?" Cleveland called to him. "Hey, Grook, the convenience!"

All the adults and most of the children looked at Cleveland. The clock yelled directions: "Two doors down! On your right!"

The weeping boy repeated the instructions to Cleveland.

A father was in the men's room, on his knees before a little girl. He was scrubbing at her skirt with a wetted paper towel. The girl looked up at Cleveland, terrified.

"Hi, darlin'," Cleveland said. "I'm just here to wash up."

"We're all through," the father stammered. He led his daughter to the door. "Mommy's out of town," he said.

"See, I told you," Cleveland heard the little girl say as the door swung closed.

He looked at himself in the mirrors over the sinks. He put on dark glasses, went into a stall, and had some straight warm brandy from a flask. He went back to the mirror. He checked the hall outside—it was empty. Back inside, in the stall, he finished the brandy in the flask.

He headed for the cafeteria. He lurched sideways and had to stop against the wall for a moment. He heard people behind him and got swiftly onto one knee. He pretended he was adjusting the heel of his shoe.

"These damn new shoes," he said.

14

The racks of overhead lights were blazing whitely. One of the scruffy teenagers pointed a huge camera on wheels at Virginia, who was talking to the man dressed as a clock. Virginia's guests, the children, were scattered all over the set. The girl in painter's pants guarded Virginia's mike cord. The floor manager, a pudgy girl in shorts, was making finger signs. Cleveland stood off with the parents and tried to see over the equipment. They watched a monitor that was on a chair seat far to the side of the action.

"Stay with us through these short announcements," Virginia said. Her theme music—a bouncy piano piece—came over the studio speakers. Cleveland noticed a second camera pointing at a brightly lit card on an easel. "Be right back," the card said. The human clock went into some shadows, took a burning cigarette from a person there, and smoked. Virginia, her face a peculiar orange, her eyebrows etched in black, squatted to chat with a little boy who was offering her a blue tablet of gum.

Cleveland moved a parent and walked over a little river of cables to stand next to Virginia.

"Fifteen seconds!" Bobby Breevort's amplified voice said. On the monitor, a commercial for a doll was winding down.

"Let's announce our wedding," Cleveland said.

"Get off," Virginia said.

Cleveland threw an arm around her. "Let's tell them all about it. You're going to be Mrs. Virginia."

"Please," she said, and pushed him.

"Five!" Breevort's voice called.

"Just an idea," Cleveland said.

As he backed off, his feet fouled in the cables and he nearly fell down. He rejoined the parents, who were giving him polite smiles.

"Hello, again," Virginia said to the camera. "Before we go to prayer corner—are we all set for prayer corner, today? For a little quiet time? A peaceful time in our busy day? Good. Before we do, I want to say hello to Beth and Megan, who're getting well in Children's Hospital. And I want to say hello to Violet, who's sitting right there." Virginia pointed at the lens. "And I want to thank her for being so wonderful. Hello, Violet."

"Hello, Miss Virginia!" Cleveland hollered in a little girl's voice.

15

I need cooler clothes," Maureen said, bustling across the kitchen.

"Hold it, hold it, wait," Lola said. "See this person?" She waved an ice-cream scoop at Violet, who was seated at the table in the breakfast room. Violet wore a beat-up, pointed hat, and her mouth had been circled with lipstick. Arranged around her placemat were cardboard animal cutouts, party napkins, a foil-covered horn. Twisted strips of crepe paper hung from the table.

"Jesus," Maureen said, "you really went all out."

"I did my bit," Lola said. "Now fork over the keys to your daddy's car. I have research to do at the language library."

"Research, my Aunt Tillie," Maureen said. "You're going on a date in those clothes." Lola was wearing a mint-green shift, nylons, T-strap shoes.

Maureen took the ice-cream scoop away from Lola and rinsed it clean at the sink. She said, "Violet's had enough white sugar for one lifetime."

"Hey, she wants it," Lola said. "And I always say trust the

body. It craves what it needs. Violet's body craves peanut-butter ice cream."

"That's what you're giving me?" Violet said. "You swore it was lemon."

"I lied," Lola said. "We don't have lemon. I don't think lemon ice cream exists."

"She lies all the time," Maureen said. "But woe be to you if *you* lie."

"Criticize away. I just took a huge raise off the boss. Double pay for the quadruple load of work I do, like nurse-maiding your child."

"See how she lies?" Maureen said, and then to Lola: "Couldn't you just watch her for one more sec, while I get on my bathing suit or something? Here." She flipped Lola the car keys and left the kitchen.

Lola dropped the keys into her tall pocketbook, which matched her shoes. She scooped ice cream for Violet and served it in a carnival glass cup.

"Let me get finished with this," she said. She sat opposite Violet at the table and lowered her eyes to a sheet of lined paper. She picked up her fountain pen.

"You promised lemon," Violet said.

"Silence," Lola said. "I'm writing a poem."

16

Virginia and Cleveland and Bobby Breevort were in the darkened cafeteria drinking milk from small cartons. Cleveland said, "Honey, I'm sorry. I didn't think they'd pick up my voice. Why not just cut that part out of the tape?"

"Actually, just for your info," Breevort said, "we have to treat a taped performance as if it were live. We can't afford to tape over or edit, so even though it doesn't look like it, we've timed everything down to the second. And unless Miss Virginia accidentally bares her chest, or one of the kids spits up on camera, or dies, we just plow ahead and show the thing as is."

"Well, I didn't know," Cleveland said, and Virginia stared at her milk. "But listen, I don't want to be insulting, darlin', I really don't, but this ain't exactly the Old Vic or anything and you weren't doing *Hamlet*. Yours is a show that only kids and their parents and preachers' wives watch and maybe a couple of insomniacs. I don't see how a granddad saying hello to his Violet or teasing you on camera a little could hurt anything."

"Well, I think you're seriously missing the point when you say that," Bobby Breevort said.

Cleveland said, "People at home watching will be delighted to see someone cutting up a little. Putting some real life in the thing. You ought to cut up more often, I think."

"What we try to do, without my being too heavy about it," Breevort said, "is we offer a professional product. We do a relatively quiet TV show, with an inspirational slant, to compete with all the slam-bang, noisy, awful, violent junk that kids get every other day of the week. I believe we do a gentle show about being gentle. And I think Ginny's offended because—"

"A professional product," Virginia said hotly. "He doesn't seem to understand that this is my job. This is my chosen work. I take it very seriously. I know the good I do, no matter how small he judges it."

"I don't say it's small. I never said that," Cleveland said.

"He didn't really say that," Breevort said.

"Shut up, Bobby. I don't interfere with his work. I don't go around wrecking business deals for him. I've never denigrated his soda-pop business," Virginia said, "or cast aspersions on his baby golf empire—both of which do people so much tremendous good."

"They don't hurt anyone," Cleveland said.

"I can't believe you would interfere so shamelessly with my professional life, or that you would act so childishly just because a camera was around. You're worse than the little children I have on, who can't refrain from yelling and waving to friends in the camera."

"I didn't do either one," Cleveland said.

Breevort said, "Really, Ginny, no major harm was done."

"Oh, yes," she said. "Oh, yes, yes, yes."

17

Cleveland took Virginia from the studio to her condominium, where she showered and changed. Then he took her to a German restaurant. He ordered martinis. He purchased and then puffed on a narrow green cigar that had been displayed in a glass case under the cash register counter. When the waitress arrived with drinks, Cleveland ordered a second round.

"Not for me," Virginia said.

"Bring them anyway," Cleveland said.

The waitress moved off.

Virginia said, "I am starving. I won't sit here starving and watch you fry your brains with that stuff. I'll leave first."

"Now let me just tell you something." Cleveland leaned close. "I won't be bullied around by a woman—not ever. It happened to me once, and it won't happen to me again. You either get your fingers out of my habits or you get yourself out of my life."

"Softer," Virginia said.

"I've got my ways. I won't apologize for them."

Virginia sat very straight and forced a smile. "All right. Let's save it."

Cleveland bashed the table with his fist. The plates and glasses jumped. The restaurant went silent. "A little order in the court," he said.

"Are you finished?" she said.

He puffed on his cigar. He chewed an olive. They were quiet for minutes. Their food order of sausages and sauerkraut came.

"Why don't we just enjoy our food?" Cleveland said.

But he sent his back, saying the meat was burned.

"Don't wait for me," he barked at her. "Eat yours if you can."

"Better," he said, when the exasperated waitress returned. He put his knife and fork to work. He ate a little and stopped.

"I'm not going to live with your family," Virginia said.

"What does that mean? Wedding's off?"

"No, but I've had a very different sort of life than you—than they all lead. I like a serene life, without a lot of noise and crowds. I'm not being unreasonable. Maureen is an adult and a mother. She's too old to be living at home. Howdy needs a life of his own."

"And you need a big house, and a live-in maid, and a solid income."

"Let's try to talk," Virginia said.

She spent half an hour explaining to him.

"I can't ask them to go," Cleveland said. "You may be right about everything, but I can't ask them to go. Not after their mother left the way she did."

"You could tell them, not ask them," Virginia said. "If you want me, you would set them loose."

"I can't," Cleveland said.

18

Walking with their feet sideways, Maureen and Violet went down into the ravine behind Violet's play yard. They doubled over and charged up the face of the ravine. Maureen made it to the crest while Violet still churned her legs in a spill of loose gravel below. Maureen stepped into a thicket of blackberries. She was carrying a plastic bucket. "Stay away from here!" she called. "It's prickly."

Violet went around the tall berry bushes to a monument-like boulder. She climbed it and looked out over a broad sweep of fairway at a water hazard that shone like gun metal in the white sun. She saw a golf cart turn and go the other way. "Can't I help?" Violet yelled.

"Help, then," Maureen yelled back. "Get all the mint leaves you can find."

Maureen worked the branches, holding the bucket to catch the berries.

"These'll be wonderful," she said.

"Jesus Christ!" Violet shouted.

"What are you saying?" Maureen yelled. She kicked her leg free and dried the sweat on her face.

"Mommy!" Violet screamed.

"What?" Maureen's heart banged. She pushed down branches to sight her daughter.

Violet screamed, "I'm stinging!"

Maureen trampled foliage, thrashing before her with the plastic bucket. She cleared the thicket and saw her daughter, who was beside the huge stone, spinning, dancing, flapping her hands. The air around Violet was dotted with black. There were wasps stuck on her legs, in her hair, on her face.

"Bees!" Violet shrieked.

Maureen swooped at her in a gallop. She punched at the air and caught up Violet's flying hand.

"Run!" Maureen screamed. They ran onto the golf course, Maureen howling curses.

A golf cart headed for them. It was pink and was covered with a fringed, gaily striped awning.

"Help!" Maureen screamed.

They sprinted fifty yards and then Violet went down. Maureen heard all the air go out of the little body in a gasp when it hit the turf, chest first. Maureen fell to get herself stopped. Violet rolled on the grass, and then lay on her belly, her mouth working, gulping for breath. Maureen froze in the sprawl of her own fall. She watched her daughter, certain that here and now they were both going to die.

The cart coasted up. The driver was a short man in crazy-quilt trousers.

"Is he sick? What should I do?" the man said. He pulled off his golfing glove and stood over Violet with his hands on his bent knees. "My gosh. What happened to his face?"

"Mommy!" Violet screamed.

Maureen was trying to talk. "Wasps," she managed.

"No problem," the man said.

"They wanted to kill us," Maureen gasped.

"Wasps?" the man said. "The bastards, they hurt like hell, don't they?"

Violet screamed, "Oh, my legs!"

"Hospital," Maureen said.

"He's going to be fine," the man said. "Let's load him into my buggy, and take him into the clubhouse, and then get somebody to whip him right over to the emergency room."

"Goddamn fucking bugs," Maureen said.

"Don't get him more upset," the man said.

"You asshole," Maureen said. "Will you hurry?"

19

Has arrelgy of insect poison," the Asian doctor said.

"She—has—an—allergy?" Maureen said.

"Arrelgy, okay?"

They were in a hallway of St. Boniface the Greater. Violet had been loaded onto a high tray, given a syringeful of something white, then wheeled off by deliberate-looking medics.

The doctor touched Maureen's shoulder and hurried away.

"Will she die?" Maureen called to his back.

She went to the admitting room and helped a blowzy receptionist type up a complicated form. The receptionist sat back in her roller chair and admired the paper, which was tangerine-colored. Maureen asked if the receptionist knew anything about wasp stings.

"I'm sure the doctor does," the receptionist said. "Have a drink of water."

Maureen waited an hour in the emergency room. She bummed cigarettes. She paced between fiberglass chairs yoked together by steel rods. She telephoned Howdy.

When he showed up, he hurried into the room right past Maureen, and stormed up to the receptionist counter. "Hey!" he called to the vacant swivel chair.

Maureen made a sharp little whistle.

"Okay," Howdy said. "I'm here."

"They say they're going to keep her awhile," Maureen said.

The woman next to Maureen sighed.

Howdy said, "I couldn't find Daddy at the TV station, and they couldn't find Lola at the library, but I got Chris and he's meeting us at the house."

"Lola?" Maureen said.

"The husband always comes apart," said the woman next to Maureen.

"He's not a husband," Maureen said.

"I should have known," the woman said.

The doctor came out through the mechanical doors. He had some charts on a clipboard, a paper box, a ballpoint pen that he snapped continuously. "Your dotta?" he said.

"My daughter," Maureen said.

"Prease?" the doctor said.

Howdy got out of his seat and the doctor sat down. He showed Maureen the hypodermic kit in the box. He explained how to use it.

"The poison of wasp build up, okay? Cumurative?"

"Is cumulative?" Maureen said.

"And so within immediately thirty minute is stung you give this? Prease? Her rungs corrapse if you don't, okay?"

Maureen put her head in her hands.

"Not to pick any more bellies," the doctor said. He held up the hypodermic. "Okay?"

20

The village green was a square with trees and lighted globes on iron poles. Cleveland saw fireflies winking over the slatted benches and in the yards of the old homes that bordered the green. He parked his Oldsmobile at a coin meter that was posted with a "Commercial Only" sign, and walked Virginia up the grass. Overhead, the sky streamed with long schools of clouds burning orange in the day's last sun. A carillon in the dark tower of the Episcopalian church bonged out an evening hymn.

"Flat," Cleveland said.

"The music?" Virginia said.

"I wouldn't know about that. I mean the world is flat," Cleveland said.

Cleveland did a slow turn, and took in the courthouse, the two churches, the old library, the tired houses, the new adobe police station.

"I would say the sky is almost gaudy tonight," Virginia said.

"Baby doll, this'd be run of the mill for a Texas sunset. When I was a kid, the world was divided in half. The earth part was where you shoved cowshit and where the pigs chewed each other and ate their babies. Everything else was sky. The sky was God's speech."

"I like that," Virginia said.

"Anything with God in it," Cleveland said.

They walked by some aluminum sheets tacked together into hut shapes. "Bennington Arts Council," Virginia read from a sign on the ground. "Works by Dina Buzzard."

"Howdy-type junk," Cleveland said. He pulled her sleeve and led her away from the sculpture.

"When I was a kid, I made hat bands from snakeskins and leather and sold them for five bucks—a fortune. I killed six snakes one afternoon with my father's Remington, hung them to rot on a tent-pole setup. I knew I was going to be a millionaire even then. I was Joseph in my third-grade Christmas thing, and I got a standing ovation. I always amazed myself."

"Are you a millionaire?" Virginia said.

"I went all over Europe in Ordnance Supply—that's passing out the cannons. It's a tiny place, Europe, like New York City. People say it's big, but it's all closed down and tiny."

"Are you really a millionaire?" Virginia said.

"I don't know. Talk to my money man. They'll tell you, they'll say, 'Now, Bob Hope is worth forty million,' and I say, 'Yeah? To whom?' You reach a place, building money, when you realize just that, and it makes you sad. You going to marry me?"

"I think I can. I'll have to adjust," Virginia said.

Cleveland said, "That's right. If it's any comfort to you, we all adjust every day of our lives. I thought I was sent from the stars. Howdy and Maureen and now you, you're all showing me I'm just another shithead. I'd marry Lola if she'd have me and if it weren't crossing the color line. She's got one foot on earth and the other down deeper than that."

"She *is* wonderful," Virginia said.

"So?" Cleveland said.

"We'll see," Virginia said.

21

Chris's car hurtled down the Cleveland drive, banging and creaking over the potholes, waffling some at the rutted corner.

He got out and tried the garage. He found the sliding glass doors off the patio locked. He pounded the blue front doors. Finally, he took a running jump at the side of the house. He got over Maureen's balcony railing and came down through the house—to Violet's bedroom.

Violet had been painted with white ointment. She lay sleeping in her bathing-suit bottom. One of her eyelids was grotesquely swollen, and her left ear was fat under the coat of white. She was brow-knitted, open-mouthed, desperate in sleep.

Chris thought better of lighting his cigarette. He sat gently on the bed, beyond Violet's feet. He watched. Violet lay cuddled into the stuffed animals that had been arranged around her shoulders.

Chris looked and looked and winced. The right leg was knotty with stings. "And where's Mom?" he muttered to himself. "This dirty family."

He tiptoed out and made his way swiftly to his car. From his back seat, he unloaded an oilcloth, a gallon can of gasoline, a plunger-action weed sprayer, rawhide gloves, a stiff cloth hat with fine-mesh netting sewn all around the brim. He took out cans of bug repellent. He sprayed the oilcloth until his nose couldn't take any more.

22

In her wet right hand, Maureen was squeezing three fingers of her wet left hand. She rocked on Howdy's sofa and counted aloud to twenty. She was sweating. Her hairline was damp. The back of her blouse was dark.

Howdy breathed into a brown paper sack. He threw the sack to his sister.

"Breathe into it," he said.

"Call someone," she said.

"It'll pass," Howdy said. He read his pulse. "Way too fast."

Maureen read her pulse. "Ditto," she said.

"What would help?" Howdy said.

"Call someone."

"Yeah, but who? Oh, God. I've got to lie down."

Howdy got onto the floor. Maureen lay face up on the sofa.

"Welcome to the twenty-first century," Howdy said.

"We're being ridiculous," Maureen said. She rolled off the sofa and did pushups and sit-ups and leg lifts.

Howdy ran in place. He chinned himself on the door frame.

They lay down again, panting. "Poor Stephanie," he said.

"That ratface," Maureen said.

"A pitiful person," Howdy said.

"I'd much rather talk about going to see Mother."

"Aer Lingus from New York or Boston to Dublin. Under three hundred apiece both ways," Howdy said.

"She knows we're coming?" Maureen said.

"I've written to her. And I've got my money together."

"It's all going to happen," Maureen said. "It's seemed so half-baked and tentative until now."

"You're thinking in the old patterns. We've got to learn to live bigger, trust ourselves to take risks. Get into the habit."

"What on earth did you write in your letter?"

Howdy jumped up and went to a drawer. He read aloud from a carbon copy.

"That's awful," Maureen said. "That sounds like a business letter. You signed it, 'Respectfully, Howard Cleveland.' "

"Well, my tactic was this—I didn't want to scare her," Howdy said.

"It sounds like you're working for the FBI. And you didn't even *mention* me."

"You're the surprise I was talking about. I only wanted to alert her, keep it simple, not freight it with anything. Me and you, the surprise."

"Yeah, like a plague," Maureen said.

"You don't see my tactic," Howdy said.

"Oh, Howdy. Why are you so odd? Why does your mind work in such twisted ways?"

"Hey!" he said.

"Well, *Jesus*. If I got a letter like that from Violet someday, I'd open my wrists without blinking. Not even, 'Warmest regards,' or 'Yours,' or 'Affectionately'?"

"I'll read it again," Howdy said. " 'Dearest Mother, I'm your son, Howard. I am going to visit Ireland soon. I plan to stop off in Donegal and would like very much to see you. I would appreciate it if you would see me. Perhaps we could have dinner together, or go to the theater. I look forward to seeing you. I have a surprise. . . .' "

"That 'surprise' sounds ominous," Maureen said. "Could be anything, but it doesn't sound like it could be me."

"We're going to have to tell Daddy soon, so we can get her

right address," Howdy said. "I also wrote, 'I hope this letter reaches you.' "

Maureen said, "Congratulations, Howdy. You started every sentence with 'I.' Very revealing."

" 'You may respond with a letter to the above street address, or telephone me.' " Howdy looked up and said, "And then I, you know, I give our phone number."

"I know."

" 'I don't expect you to call or write, however, and so am writing this letter to alert you to my coming sometime early in September. Respectfully, etc.' "

"Good Christ," Maureen said. "You creep."

23

Chris had cut a head hole and draped the sprayed oilcloth over himself like a serape. He wore his gloves and hat and carried the gas-filled weed sprayer. He looked in Violet's play yard, but he found nothing. He searched for half an hour.

He removed his netted hat and immediately spotted a wasp—it was bumping the end of one of the pipes on Violet's jungle gym. He watched. It bumped the pipe, circled, bumped again, nudging something like a smear of peanut butter.

Chris heard traffic from the faraway interstate. He heard rolling trucks. A plane moaned over in the humid twilight.

The wasp made a figure eight in the air, then zipped away. Another wasp appeared and bumped into the pipe. A third, Chris noticed with a start, crawled over the toe of his boot. There was a whirring, whining sound that faded in and out. Chris put on his hat and followed the first wasp.

The nest was in a far corner of Cleveland's toolshed, with many outlying bits of nest in the wooden coves all around it.

The central dwelling was volleyball-sized, a swollen, delicate contrivance of gray paperlike tissue.

Chris emptied the shed quickly. He flung out tools and toys. He pushed the tractor mower off into the yard.

He was stung three times through his jeans. He was limping when he went back into the shed.

Chris soaked the nest with gasoline. A plume of the misted fuel drifted and condensed on his serape, more collected on his boots. He dropped the sprayer and picked up the can. His wrist tickled between cuff and glove. There were two wasps there which he smashed to paste. A minute later their poison made him think he had broken his arm.

He ran a trail of gas out the door and twenty yards into the lawn. He tossed the can back inside. From his pocket, he took his cigarette lighter.

"Here comes hell!"

He caught fire before the shed did. His oilcloth serape blew a white flame up at his face. He rolled in the high, rain-drenched grass. The explosion came—much louder, much more violent than he had expected. The blaze from the shed went thirty feet into the air and the building snapped and roared.

Chris sat up and chuckled. He watched the toolshed go.

24

World War Three," Howdy said.

"That was close," Maureen said.

They hurried downstairs, across the lawn to the house, and ran around the house to the back.

"Holy God!" Howdy said.

"What's that?" Maureen said.

Chris, draped in the tablecloth and still wearing his bee hat, was limping away from the inferno. He yanked off his gloves and slammed them to the ground.

"He may be dangerous," Howdy said.

"Are you dangerous?" Maureen called. "Going to blow up the house next?"

Chris threw his hat on the grass. He looked at his wrist. He pulled off the tablecloth and sat down in a squat. His fingers shook.

Howdy said, "Dad's going to break wide open when he sees this. He's going to come after you, Chris."

"I care," Chris said.

Howdy moved closer to the fire. "It's beautiful. I've got to say that much," he said.

"You did it this time," Maureen said. "You did it and tied a ribbon around it. Daddy'll kill you for this."

Chris said, "Maureen, what were you and Howdy doing? You left Violet alone? Where were you? Lying in a puddle somewhere talking about Mommy?"

"Of course not," Maureen said. "Violet is sedated. There's nothing I could do but watch her sleep."

"I want Violet," Chris said. "And I frankly think I could get her. I don't trust you to be around her. Not you or any of your family. You people are not responsible enough, not mentally or physically or anything."

"What the hell are you talking about?" Maureen said.

"Case in point." Chris nodded at Howdy, who was smiling broadly at the blaze.

Maureen sighed and nodded. She sat on the grass beside Chris. "You smell very bad," she said.

"I caught on fire," he said.

"I'm going to see my mother. Nothing will stop me."

Chris said, "Not with Violet, you're not. Unless you want to take me with you. I've got the rest of my prize money to pay my way."

"Fine," Maureen said.

"Fine," Chris said. "It's settled."

"Yes, it's settled," Maureen said. "You'll come with us. Actually, it's a good idea because I didn't really trust Howdy to handle everything."

Chris said, "The trip could be a honeymoon."

"Why not?" Maureen said. "Marrying you is no different than not marrying you."

"Don't try to act nuts, Maureen. You do it well enough without trying. I swear I can't keep up with you. Here I am burning up six different ways, and I can't even tell if you're serious."

"Neither can I," she said, and sighed. "But, Chris? I do admire you for burning down the toolshed. Sometimes, I guess, the admiration I feel for you is love, like. Or maybe not. Anyway, I can't picture myself with anyone else."

"You lack imagination," Chris said. "Don't you know how come I torched the toolshed?"

"It doesn't matter," Maureen said, and sighed again. "It's a symbol."

"Jesus," Chris said. "Jesus goddamn Christ."

25

Cleveland stopped at a Frigid Twist for chocolate cones. Dusty baseball players on racing bikes swept around the parking lot in big circles. One, who had a brown stick of candy stuck in his mouth like a cigar and his fielder's mitt on his head, yelled, "Hey, homo!" at Cleveland.

Whistling without music between licks at his cone, Cleveland drove off, heading homeward. He savored the quiet cabin of his big automobile. Virginia was sweetly, gently raking his bare steering arm with her pretty nails. She made small, white lines on his tan.

A hook and ladder truck, an ambulance van, and a constable's car were moving in file out Cleveland's drive.

"Be calm," he said to Virginia.

She said, "They aren't using their flashers, and they're leaving, not coming."

"So you can be calm," he said. "I mean, I guess it's all burned down already."

The passenger in the constable's car, a young man in a cop's hat, saluted them jauntily.

Cleveland sped up the drive and jogged into the house by way of the kitchen door. Howdy was in the breakfast room, his elbows to either side of a glass of buttermilk.

"Give it to me slow," Cleveland said.

"Violet's sleeping. All's well," Howdy said.

"Well, sonny, I want you to know I just ran into your guests in the big red trucks."

"I know. I bet it took some years off you."

Cleveland said. "You fetch my automatic pistol so I can kill you or somebody once and for all."

"Chris, you mean," Howdy said, and then he told his story.

26

Chris was watching television with Maureen. He wore one of Cleveland's bathrobes and a big, complicated, torn-sheet-and-masking-tape bandage on his raised shin. He said, "I'll talk," but Cleveland moved quickly out of the room. Virginia followed him without saying a word. She didn't glance at Maureen or Chris. Howdy moseyed in from the kitchen, yawning.

"What's this?" Howdy said, looking at the TV.

"Nothing," Maureen said.

"Just excrement," Chris said.

Howdy got down, cross-legged, and watched with them. "Daddy's not mad," he said. "He's trying to be, but he's really not."

"That's a surprise," Maureen said.

"Every now and then, your father and I understand each other," Chris said. "Or at least we have a sort of sympathetic reaction to life."

"Ha!" Howdy said.

"Makes sense," Maureen said.

27

Violet looked terrible. The unguent on her ear and eyelid had dried and cracked, making the flesh seem broken in the light that came from the hall. She groaned in her sleep.

Virginia watched without expression.

Cleveland sat on the bed and moved Violet's limbs, studying them. He brushed a little band of damp hair from her cheek and she whimpered.

"It's all right," he said.

She turned onto her back and made a circle with her arms, wanting to be picked up.

Cleveland stroked her forehead until she slept soundly again.

"Not bad," he said.

"You come with me," Virginia said. She took him to his bedroom. "I'm so angry I could weep," she said. "Did you see what I saw? That child—that dear child—stung and distorted even while she sleeps. Where is her mother?"

"You know where Mo is."

"Yes. Not with her child. Watching TV. She's hysterical and egocentric and thoroughly irresponsible."

"Let me get on a light," Cleveland said.

"No! I don't want to see your face. This family is a mess. It's my fault I'm not loving enough or good enough to help here. But I'm not. It's too big a mess, and too painful for me."

Cleveland said, "A bad week, is all. You caught us with our pants down."

Virginia heaved three great courage-giving breaths. "It isn't the chaos," she said. "It's the hopelessness. Your family's situation is hopeless because there isn't enough intelligence here. Not one of you can save himself or stop himself from harming the others because you just don't *think*. You have lost the habit of thinking."

"I see," Cleveland said.

They went silently into the kitchen together. Virginia put a kettle of water on the stove. She worked cupboards and pantry shelves, took down cans and boxes, considered them, and put them back.

"No one's fault," Cleveland said. "The wasps."

"It's everyone's fault. Everybody involved botched up. I can tell you how, from step one, everyone botched up."

Cleveland said, "Is that what you've been doing? Tallying errors? Adding up the various stupidities of my stupid family?"

Cleveland went a few steps off toward the dining room.

"I don't care if they can hear me," Virginia called after him. "Just don't tell me to lower my voice."

"Who said anything about lowering your voice?"

"I just want some tea," she said.

He came back. "Help yourself to tea. Help yourself to yelling and tea drinking."

"I warned you not to tell me to lower my voice."

"Who said anything about it? Me? I didn't. I said help yourself. Bust a lung. Scream out," he said.

"I wasn't screaming."

"But do. *Do*. And drink a million gallons of tea. A jillion gallons."

"I wasn't screaming," she said.

"Who said you were?"

"I wasn't."

"Who said you were?"

"I don't care if they hear me."

"Do you think I care?" Cleveland said. "I don't care. I think you're right. We *are* a stupid family."

"I didn't say that."

Cleveland said, "Just because Howdy and Maureen did so well on placement tests and IQ tests in high school that their teachers wanted to skip them up to college, just because of *that,* I don't think we're smart."

"Those tests mean nothing," Virginia said.

"Who said they did? *I* didn't. Just because I built myself from a redneck Okie into a billionaire businessman, that doesn't take any intelligence, either. You think I don't know that?"

"Making money doesn't prove—"

"While *you* run around in public dressed up like a gingerbread girl because *that's* intelligent. Playing with Grook the Clock on the goddamn television box, which no one watches on Sunday morning except the mentally bankrupt."

"You drunken sinner. Don't raise your hand to me."

"I was just going for the bottle of rye, sweetheart."

"You're not drinking another swallow in my presence," Virginia said.

"I wasn't reaching it down to drink it but to bang you on the snout with it."

"Hey," Maureen said.

"What is it?" Cleveland said.

Maureen skidded between him and Virginia to the refrigerator.

"Ham sandwich," she said.

"Get out," Cleveland said.

Maureen did an abrupt about-face.

"That's all, brother," Virginia said.

"Good," Cleveland said.

"You are repugnant, disgusting, perfectly ridiculous."

"Good."

"I will pray for you."

"Good."

"I will pray for you and your children."

"Great. Bye now."

"There's no power that can restore you."

"Bye-bye. So long. Good."

"You are not a man. You don't talk like a man."

"Good, good, good," Cleveland said. He put his fingers into his ears and squeezed his eyes shut.

Four

1

Bathed, sober, and sipping carrot juice, Cleveland spent his morning in the study. He spoke on the phone with his insurance agent, caught up with his business mail, and, in longhand, drafted replies to be typed by his secretary downtown. He read and initialed memos and clipped the papers together. From a drawer, he pulled a computer printout headed "Revised Personnel List." He was wrestling with the list when Lola brought him a lunch tray with red caviar, cheese, coffee.

"My stars, it's the niggra," he said.

"You seem chipper enough for a case of advanced senility," she said, setting the tray on his desk.

"I'm rethinking your indenture. Sit down," he said.

"You always want me to sit down. I guess so you can look up my dress."

"No, you never wear a dress. I want to look *down* your blouse."

"Nothing to see in that direction."

"You're in a good mood, too," he said.

"I had a date."

"Your friend from the university?"

"That's the one," Lola said.

Cleveland rattled the printout. He used a ruler and a marker pen to make a line on the page.

"This is you," he said.

"Turtlidge, L.," Lola read. "That's me, all right."

"You know that you are in the corporation, with profit sharing and insurance breaks and all?"

"I know they pay me sometimes," she said.

"They *always* do—even when it's one of my checks. And now they'll pay you double the underlined figure on that sheet, and you'll have twice the vacation plan, and I'm throwing in two more shares of Whistle-Low, and do you know what a share is selling for now?"

"Lord, Lord."

"I'm not joking. I'm fixing it this afternoon."

"My savior."

"And before you fumble over some sorry kind of thank you, I'll tell you it doesn't mean piss to me, I'm so rich."

"How nice," Lola said. She stood and handed back the paper.

"Oh, you'll spend it unwisely and get in hot water with the IRS and curse me in the end," he said.

"That's the truth," Lola said.

She left him, and he called, "It's not from my pockets, Turtlidge, L. It's from the coffers of the company, which are bottomless! All it'll mean is that the price of my cream sodas goes up another dime!"

2

Howdy was shirtless. He was putting a good two-coat wax job on his MG. Sweat ran off him as he moved the rag in swirls. Every so often, he straightened and stepped back to study the work. Once when he did this, he stumbled on Maureen, who lay on a towel on the blacktop with her face aimed at the overhead sun.

Howdy hitched up his chinos and set to work on the other side of the hood.

Maureen said, "Ow."

"Just feeling it, huh?"

"You kicked me," she said.

"Your body's just someplace else, huh?" he said.

"They have greyhound racing six nights a week in Dublin," Maureen said.

"We'll go every night."

"But there are hardly any trees in the whole country," she said. "Only one-fortieth of the country has trees."

"Who needs trees?" Howdy said. He flapped and turned the rag over, and then left it on the car to look around at the elms, the sycamore, the butternut and poplar trees.

A stray cat with something alive in its teeth galloped from the copse that surrounded the statue of the nymph.

"What do you think about Dad and Virginia splitting up?"

"He deserves a Nobel prize."

"Why didn't we like her? Why did we hate Virginia?"

"You're the older brother. You don't know?"

"I am?" Howdy said. "Oh, *older*, yeah, I am. But, I mean, I guess I keep forgetting why I didn't like her." He walked around the car once and started back to buffing. "You know, I've never enjoyed talking to you."

Maureen said, "We didn't like her because she didn't like us."

"Violet!" Howdy said. "Do not chase that cat!"

"What's she doing?"

"Chasing a cat."

"Don't chase it, dear!" Maureen yelled, without moving.

"Why not?" Violet trotted up, short of breath.

"It was eating," Howdy said.

"So?"

"So, it was eating a birdie. Eating its guts and eyeballs, which you don't want to watch it do," Howdy said.

"Who says I don't?"

"Did it really have a bird?" Maureen said.

Howdy puffed and made his scrubbing motion. "Had something," he said.

"You're making a shadow, baby," Maureen said. "Honey? Move away."

Violet had more or less recovered from the wasp stings. She hadn't wanted to play outside, though, until the Whier children—the children closest in the neighborhood—had come to collect her. She had been fearlessly running in the front yard ever since.

"Tommy Whier is still sneaking peeks at you, Mo," Howdy said. "He's over in the lilacs, slobbering."

"The swine," Maureen said. She checked the halter of her bikini.

"I hate him," Violet said.

"That's wise," Maureen said.

"I hate him too," Howdy said.

"I wouldn't mind betting the dogs in Dublin," Maureen said.

Violet lay down beside her mother.

"Go noodle around with the Whiers," Maureen said.

"I hate them all," Violet said.

Howdy finished burnishing the second coat of wax. He spritzed the headlights with soapy water from a plastic bottle and wiped them with a clean rag. Maureen turned onto her stomach. Violet tore the packaging from four small blocks of bubble gum and ate all four.

"Zzzzz," went Howdy, imitating a dentist's drill. Violet's cheeks were blown up by all the gum. Her lips were pressed out, and when she smiled, saliva ran.

"Give me one," Maureen said.

Violet stuffed a piece of gum into her mother's hand and

flipped one up to Howdy, who snatched it on the fly and said, "Good arm."

"Before you, we had a dog that was named Walter," Maureen said. She munched her gum to get it under control.

"Old Walter, that's right," Howdy said.

"And he could chew gum and blow bubbles."

"You had to put a rubber band around his nose to make him do it," Howdy said. He was chewing furiously, racing Maureen to soften the gum and inflate the first bubble.

"You remember wrong," Maureen said. "The rubber band was for something different."

Violet spat her gum into her palm. "Where is he?"

"Walter?" Howdy said. "Long dead."

"Long, long," Maureen said.

"I'll show you his grave," Howdy said.

Violet said, "Okay."

Five olive-drab helicopters, flying low and in a pattern, zoomed over the carriage house.

"Maneuvers," Howdy said. He had gotten into his car, one leg still out, and was dusting the dash. Maureen heard his gum snap.

"Beat you," he said.

Violet rested her bright pink wad carefully on the blacktop and said, "Watch this for me, will you, please?"

"She's just a list of demands," Maureen said as Violet sprinted away.

"Two more years and she'll want you to watch her divorce papers."

Maureen made a bubble, cracked it, and said, "Yep."

"Did you ever have a song in your head that wouldn't go away?" Howdy said.

"All the time," Maureen said.

"For like a *month*? You find yourself walking to the beat and chewing to the beat and doing everything just the way the rhythm goes."

"I wish this driveway were my bed," Maureen said.

"It's never a song you like."

"True," Maureen said.

"It's always a Connie Francis song."

"Or the theme of a TV show," Maureen said.

"Exactly," Howdy said. "It's a song you don't even *know*."

"Right," Maureen said.

Howdy hummed the theme from "Father Knows Best."

"I wish I were in my bed," Maureen said.

They chewed their gum in silence awhile, and then Maureen began to hum the theme from "My Three Sons."

"That's it," Howdy said. He got out of the car. "Man, look at the job I did. I really did a job."

"Wonderful," Maureen said.

"You didn't even look."

"Mind's eye," Maureen said.

"I sure did make it clean," Howdy said with pride.

3

Cleveland was still at his desk, poking holes in the blotter with a pen, when Lola stepped in and announced dinner. He pulled himself up from the leather chair and executed a few stretching exercises. His bones clicked.

He found Howdy in the breakfast room. Howdy was filling soup plates with reddish liquid from the canister of a ten-speed blender. He said, "Gazpacho."

"Let's consult the wine cellar," Cleveland said to Lola. She was in a nice cook's apron. Opposite the range, on a shelf, was a flimsy, nine-slotted wine rack that Howdy had built from pine and metal rods.

Violet, whose plate was loaded with cheese-stuffed celery

stalks and corn chips, was already busily eating at the dining room table. Maureen joined her.

"Let me, Grandpa," Violet said, hopping out of her chair and rushing to the kitchen.

Cleveland had a butterfly corkscrew he was driving into the top of a bottle of California Médoc. He got the bit completely buried in the cork before he allowed Violet to push down the gadget's handles. The extraction made a nice small sound.

"Gazpacho," Howdy said, serving Maureen and Lola. He had a bouquet of parsley, and he wouldn't let anyone eat until he'd clipped chunks of it onto the soup with a pair of kitchen shears.

"You made the soup, right?" Maureen said.

"From a recipe by Vincent Price," Howdy said.

"I wish Vincent Price could have come over and wiped up the kitchen for you. There was stuff on the ceiling," Lola said.

"I couldn't find the top of the blender," Howdy said.

"There are carrots and garlic stuck on the ceiling," Lola said.

"It'll taste good, though," Howdy said, sniffing with his nose over his bowl.

"I don't like it," Violet said.

"I don't either," Cleveland said. "It tastes like Youngstown."

"It's an acquired taste," Maureen said.

"What does that really mean?" Cleveland said. "It seems to me you could *acquire* a taste for anything, but who'd want to?"

"Well, that's your problem right there," Howdy said.

Cleveland tipped some wine into his glass. "I got a problem?" he said.

"No class," Howdy said.

"There's ice in my soup," Maureen said.

"There's supposed to be," Howdy said. "You've got no

class either. Nobody wants to try anything a little different around here."

"Give it a rest," Lola said.

"Barbarians," Howdy said.

"There's the paper," Maureen said in response to a bump at the front door. "Violet?"

"Okay, Mom," Violet said wearily.

She brought Cleveland the paper and a pair of black-framed glasses, which he hitched over his ears.

"You going to read at the table?" Howdy said.

"What's wrong with that?" Violet asked.

"Shut up," Howdy said. "You don't know what we're talking about, Vi."

"We weren't talking about anything," Cleveland said. He reached around his newspaper, picked up his wine glass, returned it after a moment, empty.

"She was just asking," Maureen said.

"Don't be so testy about your gaucho soup," Lola said. "So long as *you* like it, that's all that counts."

"This is just like my goddamn play," Howdy said in exasperation. "You all don't understand something, so you make wisecracks about it. I feel so alone sometimes. And it's not gaucho soup, Lola."

"Just you and a bunch of slobs," Cleveland said.

"That's right," Howdy said.

"We just aren't up to your standards," Cleveland said, and rustled his newspaper.

"Go ahead and make fun," Howdy said. "Be brutes."

"Were you supposed to use so many cucumbers in this soup, Howdy? With the peel still on? I'm just asking," Maureen said.

"Yes," Howdy said. "Yes, yes, yes."

"I was just asking," Maureen said.

"This tastes like trash in the disposal," Violet said.

"Try a little more before you decide," Maureen said. "Maybe you'll think of something worse."

"If it kills her, I take no responsibility," Cleveland said from behind his newspaper.

Lola snorted.

"It'll give you class, Violet," Maureen said. "If you live through it."

Howdy said, "It's a serious problem for me. I feel I can't talk to any of you. I try to make you all something nice and something new. Sometimes, I don't think you're smart enough to appreciate me."

Cleveland shot the newspaper into a corner, causing Violet to jump. "Now look, boy," he said, "you made a bad dish, pure and simple. Maybe you left something out or maybe Vincent Price was playing a little joke on you, but this is no good." Cleveland turned his bowl of gazpacho upside down. It ran a little way toward the side of the table and stopped. "I don't want to hear any more talk about the lack of intelligence in me or my family ever again."

"People sure throw a lot of food around for me to blot up in this intelligent household," Lola said.

Cleveland turned over Maureen's soup bowl and then Violet's. "Now let's continue eating," he said.

Cleveland turned away from the table, and then he turned back to them. "What are you?" he said. "Because you aren't my kids, and you aren't adults, and you aren't anything that anyone could respect or love. What are you doing in my house when every day you break my heart? Looking at you, day after day, I feel pity and even horror. Yes, I do. And, above all else, disappointment. You let me down in dozens of ways—hundreds of ways, and you've been doing it every day of your lives. Did either of you ever think of that? You'd better—both of you—find a true course and stick to it, and stop destroying your own father."

Maureen was trembling. Her fingers went up and covered her mouth.

Howdy stood abruptly, knocking over his chair. "Okay, Daddy," he said.

Cleveland stared at him. "Okay what?" Cleveland said.

"Mother," Maureen said.

"That's right," Howdy said. "We're going to our mother. We forgive her and we'll never forgive you."

"You poor children," Cleveland said. "How did I raise such fools?"

Howdy said, "We've been planning it, Mo and me."

"I want out of here," Maureen said. "I want out of everything."

"There's no way out of life," Cleveland said. He slumped into his chair. "Your mother is dead, you two. She's been dead for years. She had a cancer in her stomach and she wasn't right in the head. She was *never* right in the head. You must have known she was sick. She was never a factor in your lives. Praise God, she never wanted to be. She was an insane woman who lost all her teeth. She didn't go back to Ireland. She went to a mental institution downstate and when I'd visit her she didn't know who I was. All she ever asked for was Coke and chocolate and cigarettes. Those were the things she cared about, and not either of you. I thought you knew this stuff. I thought you never said anything, but that you knew all about it. If you'd gone to see her, she wouldn't have known who you were. She would have asked you for a Hershey bar, is all. I thought you were smart enough to figure all this out."

A low, growling moan came from outside. Cleveland, Lola, Howdy, Maureen, and Violet turned to look at the window, where Chris had his face mashed against the screen.

"It's Dad!" Violet said.

"I'm trying to fit through these little holes," Chris said. "But I'm afraid it's too much of a strain. Do you get it? A strain?"

4

The golf shoes were white suede with brown saddles so highly polished they seemed lacquered in the moonlight. Maureen used the chromed spikes on the soles to rake the tenth green. The shoes were her father's. She shuffled along inside them, leaving scars on the grass behind.

"Golf is hard," she said.

Chris was lying on his side on the ground.

"Let's make golf easier," she said.

She used the shoes to tear up the cup and make a big hole.

Chris said, "When you're done, I think you should rip out that sapling over there."

Maureen found the little spruce and tore it out of the ground. She was wrestling with a young birch that was her own height when Chris said, "Why don't you lay off that particular guy?"

Maureen stopped fighting the tree. She leaned against it with all her weight and got the tree over on its side.

Chris rolled over and patted the grass three times. "That's a pin," he said.

Maureen was dirty. Her clothes were torn. There were thorn scratches on her arms and legs. She had marched back and forth over her father's roses on her way to the golf course. She had twigs and leaves tangled in her hair.

"You're overdoing it," Chris said.

"Think so? What if your mom just died?"

Chris rolled over again, and cradled his head in his clasped fingers, face to the stars.

Maureen headed off for the country club.

Trotting, Chris caught up with her. She led him to a bike path and they followed it to the swimming pool. Racks of powerful lights blazed down on a temporary stand of bleachers. A crowd of parents in colorful clothes sat shoulder to shoulder waiting for the next event. The green water was still, but it floated wiggling stripes of reflected light neatly divided into four lanes. At the end of each lane, on a numbered wooden box, a boy stood poised to dive.

"*Bang*!" Maureen yelled from behind a section of Cyclone fence. One kid hit the water and a lot of angry faces turned in Maureen's direction. She followed a walk along some practice greens and passed a squadron of rental carts.

The lounge was open. It was a big empty room with Campbell plaid carpeting, scarlet walls, and framed copies of hunting prints.

"Judas Priest," said the bartender as Maureen took a stool and kicked off her shoes.

"Pernod," she said.

"Don't make me laugh," the bartender said.

"Another asshole," Maureen said.

Chris took the stool next to hers. He ordered a glass of ice.

"Is this Mo Cleveland?" the bartender said.

"I hate an educated bartender," Chris said.

The bartender showed Chris a black Louisville Slugger he kept by the rinsing sink.

"I see," Chris said. "You want to see mine?"

"Out," the bartender said.

"Not out," Chris said.

"Shut up," Maureen said. "Both shut up."

"My name is Bill Death," the bartender said.

Maureen took a bottle of bourbon and went to a booth.

"That can't be done," the bartender said. "You can't take that bottle. Could you get her to bring back the bottle?"

"Charge it," Chris said. "She just lost her mother."

"I don't care if she just lost Michigan, get that bottle back from her."

"I'm not getting the bottle for anyone," Chris said.

Maureen stood up and threw the bottle at the bartender. Chris caught it. "Your problem's solved," he said. He poured bourbon into his glass of ice and carried the glass out, trailing Maureen.

"You can't take a drink out of this room!" the bartender called. He started after them, gripping his Louisville Slugger.

The three of them hurried, single file, through the empty lobby of the country club. The bartender, behind Chris, raised his bat.

5

Howdy was talking to a curtain in his apartment. "Haven't I come a long way?" he asked the curtain.

His kitchen phone rang and Howdy excused himself. He went to the telephone and lifted the receiver and immediately set it back down. "That was no one," he said.

"Are you sure that was no one?" he said in a falsetto.

"Of course I'm sure," he answered. "Where was I? Oh, yeah, how long a way I've come. The last time I lost a loved one—"

"Stephanie?" he asked in falsetto.

"Right. When I lost old Steph, I broke this place to pieces, and now I've lost someone else and instead of breaking things, I've decided to repair all the earlier damage as a constructive way of dealing with grief. I call that coming a long way."

The phone rang again. In the falsetto voice, he said, "You'd better get it. That would be the mature thing."

He went to the kitchen and picked up the receiver. "Hello?"

"Signoracci," a girl's voice said. "Tits."

"Yeah," Howdy said.

"How do you like it for a first name? New name, new image."

"Tits Signoracci?" Howdy said.

"Sticks in the mind," she said.

"It's clever," Howdy said with no interest.

The girl said, "We're going all the way this time or fuck it. We found a kid from Detroit with a hand-held probe synthesizer. Knocks them on their gourds. He shaves his head, the kid. I shaved mine, too."

"Sounds good," Howdy said.

"We've got like five o'clock shadow, you know? Did I forget our boots?"

"Bigger boots?" Howdy said.

"Crueler boots," the girl said. "Like for kicking in heads. Made in England. We make a fucking good gig. People go nuts."

"Which people?"

Signoracci said, "The audience, man. We did a gig at the Jewish Center."

"Now you're talking," Howdy said.

Signoracci said, "You could smell it, man. People were really torn up. I got fucking pulled off the *stage*."

"Maybe I'll hear you sometime."

"Fucking right," the girl said. "So what are you doing?"

"Talking to myself and answering back in a different voice."

"Yeah, I like to do that all the time," she said. "I can really get into it. Like, sometimes, I become a guy who's coaxing myself into doing something knobby."

"Yeah," Howdy said.

"I really freak, man."

"I've just wrapped the phone cord around my neck about eight times," Howdy said.

"I do that too."

"I'm looking at a jar of Hellman's," Howdy said. "I'm in my kitchen."

"I'm in my bathroom, looking at a box of Light Days."

"My mother's dead," Howdy said. "I didn't really think

I'd tell you that. Now I'm looking at a bottle of Louisiana Hot Sauce."

"I wish you hadn't told me about your mom. It's none of my business. I, anyway, don't believe anybody really dies all the way. That's just crap."

"Who does vocals besides you? The Detroit guy?" Howdy asked.

The girl said. "Yeah. I mean, he's doing it. Sounds like nobody I can think of. So you're handling this thing about your mom and just working it out?"

Howdy said, "If I dropped to my knees and you screamed into the phone, all the wire around my throat carrying your voice would choke me to death. Maybe there's a song in that for you."

"No, man," the girl said. "My voice would keep you alive, even if your heart didn't get oxygen and stuff. It's just energy. You know, you're out of the group."

"I guessed that," Howdy said.

"It's more like you quit than like I'm saying get out. But this time we're going for it all. You were holding us back, and we didn't realize it."

"I'm sorry," Howdy said.

He hung up the phone. He took the cord from around his neck and began to assemble his apartment. First, he collected all the shards of broken glass and made a pile of them on top of the television. He turned on the set. He sat down and watched. He watched until he fell asleep.

6

The drink," the bartender said, behind them. "Give me back the drink or I'll knock it out of your hand."

Chris turned and emptied his glass on the bartender and

then he hurt him with a left. Maureen sprinted for the doors. Chris caught up with her, and they walked together through the parking lot. They handed a cigarette back and forth. Maureen sprinted off again. This time Chris stayed where he was.

She kept on the grass because she was barefoot. An hour's walk took her to a picnic park that ran beside the Skheenough River. The park closed officially at dusk. Maureen stayed in the shadows to avoid prowl cars. Out on the wide slow river, a police boat trawled and now and then played a spotlight over the shore.

She walked another hour. Her legs gave out and she sat on a bench. She clawed at the bites on her ankles.

There was a bridge in her view, massive in the dark, that groaned and sang with intermittent traffic. Small craft were tied up in quiet lines at a boat slip.

From behind her, a voice said, "So what's your story?"

A small sun ignited in her face.

Maureen said, "I want a cigarette."

She was given a cigarette and a lighter. She snapped the lighter and saw the patrolman. He was a short, featureless shape in the dark.

"Have you been attacked?" he said.

"Death in the family. My mom. Just trying to walk it off."

"Walk it off somewhere else," the patrolman said.

Maureen started crying in a brand-new way.

"I'm sorry," the patrolman said. He withdrew into the shadows. He returned and gave her a folded square of paper, a perfumed towelette.

"Wash 'N' Dry," he said.

Maureen mopped her face.

The park patrolman ran up the aerial on his walkie-talkie and croaked into the box. Most of what he said was numbers. He stood away from Maureen, who smoked the cigarette to the filter.

A silver car with a side-mounted spotlight came up fast. Its braking back tires scuffed gravel. The driver had a brief conference with the patrolman and then gave Maureen the once-over with his flashlight.

"It's home or else," he said.

Maureen got into the car, which was immaculate but smelled of fish. The driver spoke into his radio—more numbers—then asked Maureen her address.

She said, "It's Eleven Barnstable Court. But you don't know where that is because it's a new street just put in for two new houses that were just built. My husband and I just moved in. The way to get there is to go to the River Twin Drive-In. It's not far from there, and then I'll walk the rest of the way because the road's not paved yet and it tears off mufflers."

The driver, who was young and wore aviator glasses, drove much too fast for Maureen. They rode in silence, then slid to a stop under the marquee for the drive-in theater.

"Where do I go?" the driver said.

"All the way in to the back row."

"That's where you live?"

"No, but there's a bunch of trees around a little gully and then on the other side are the new houses. I'm saving you ten minutes doing it this way."

The driver sighed, dropped his gear stick, and went through the ticket gate. From a projection booth that looked like a bunker, light sprayed in a fan that trapped insects. On the enormous rectangle, Clint Eastwood clenched his jaw muscles.

The driver cut his car sideways, into the last row. He threw his spotlight on the border of trees, to a house beyond.

"See?" Maureen said. "That's it."

The driver said, "That's an uninhabited house. No one lives there."

"It's pathetic, I know, but we're just starting out," Maureen said, and popped open her door.

She hid among the cars and speakers. She didn't look back to see if the patrol car stayed or gave up and left. She settled on the ground next to a station wagon loaded with teenage boys. She watched Clint Eastwood squint his eyes.

"How about a beer?" one of the boys called down to her.

"Hey, cootie. Hey, roach," one of the other boys said.

"Like a beer?" said the first boy again.

"Idiots," Maureen said.

Something flew from the car and landed ten feet from her. It was a beer can.

"Cootie," the first boy said.

"Fucking pipe down," Maureen said.

7

Cleveland spat out the grounds that he had taken in with the last of his last cup of coffee. He slumped, propping his head with fists under cheekbones. He didn't look up when Chris came in.

"I'm making breakfast," Chris said. "You know it's already four? I'll sleep in Violet's room when I'm through eating. I want to be there when she gets up."

He found eggs and a package of bacon. "Where's bread?"

Cleveland shrugged. "How the hell should I know?"

"In your own house, you don't know? Where would you look for butter?"

"Try the cupboard," Cleveland said.

"You're kidding. You think you keep butter in a cupboard?"

"Did I say that?" Cleveland said.

Chris was rooting around in the refrigerator. He found

a soup bowl in plastic wrap. "Is this chip dip? What is this orange stuff?"

"Wake Lola up and ask her," Cleveland said.

Chris heated a frying pan and laid in bacon. While it was cooking, he sipped from the bowl of orange food. "Holy God, gazpacho! It's dynamite!" He swallowed it down, scrambled eggs in the bacon fat, made toast, and a new pot of coffee.

"Whatever chance I had with my children, I lost last night," Cleveland said. "I can't be their father anymore. They don't want me to be, and I don't blame them."

"They won't forgive you," Chris said. "I'd never count on it if I were you."

"You have to help them now," Cleveland said.

"Don't need help," Chris said. "I wish there were some parsley for this soup."

"You're in charge."

"Sure," Chris said.

"I'm out of it."

"That's for the best," Chris said.

"If you'd seen their mother," Cleveland said.

"*They* should have," Chris said.

Birdsong came through the window. Cleveland got slowly to his feet. He walked around in the kitchen, took down a bottle of Scotch, put it away.

He went far back into the house and sat at the desk in his office for a couple of hours. When the sun was up, he went into his front yard and stood around. After a time, he walked off toward Howdy's place.

Howdy's television was on. He had worked through the night, constructing broken furniture and books and plates into peculiar heaps. Cleveland had to duck under a stretched canvas that Howdy had jammed crosswise into his empty hall. Howdy was in a kind of tent made of bed sheets and clothesline, with coffee table parts for struts.

"Chris loved your soup," Cleveland said.

"Good," Howdy said.

"I don't know," Cleveland said. He sat, balancing on the edge of the sofa bottom. Howdy had flipped the sofa over again. They sat in silence. Howdy fell asleep in his tent.

Cleveland reached for the television and turned up the sound. Virginia was on the screen.

"Who's done something good for another person?"

A kid's voice said, "I took brownies to a lady who's dying. Like for my mom."

"And has anyone ever done something they weren't supposed to do?" Virginia asked. There was a lot of laughter from the kids. "How do you feel when you do something bad?" Virginia said.

"When I get punished," a kid's voice said, and the shot changed to include the children, "I know my mama's doing it for my own good."

"Let's talk about dads," Virginia said. "Have you ever thought about all the things daddies do for us?"

A voice offscreen that Cleveland recognized as the clock's said, "I know a thing. They go to work and fight all that terrible traffic."

"Aren't they wonderful?" Virginia said.

Cleveland looked at his sleeping son.

8

Violet, on her way to the bathroom, tripped over Chris, who was asleep on the rug. He righted himself and blinked. He had used a stuffed bear for a pillow, and his neck hurt.

"Breakfast for you," he said.

"Lola's not around," Violet said. "Can I have Cocoa Puffs?"

In the kitchen, Chris took the glass pot from the electric

brewer and drank all the rest of the coffee. He smoked a cigarette while Violet ate her cereal. He went with her to her bathroom and supervised the washing of her face, the brushing of her teeth, the combing of her hair. Together they straightened her room, which was a chaos of clothes and toys and midget furniture. He argued with her briefly about which clothes she would wear for the day, advocating shorts and a T-shirt over Violet's choice of a swimsuit. She yielded to him, and he left her to dress. As he closed the door, he heard her say, "Shit."

Going down the hall, he heard Cleveland in his room being busy at something.

Chris cleaned up the kitchen, loaded and ran the dishwasher. He carried out two sacks of trash, and on his way back to the house snapped a bunch of blooming zinnias. He put them in a pitcher on the counter.

Lola came in with Violet behind her. "Elves have been at work," Lola said.

"You name it," Chris said. "Eggs, poached or soft or coddled. You want waffles?"

Lola reached for the coffee can.

"Sit down. I'll do it," Chris said. "There's the Sunday paper. Pay attention to the world."

9

Lola read an article about Indira Gandhi.

"That whore," she said, and turned the page.

10

Cleveland mashed socks into the corners of his suitcase and snapped the valise closed.

He lay down between his luggage and the headboard. "Sleep," he said, and shut his eyes.

11

Maureen was in the garage. She lay curled on the back seat of Cleveland's Oldsmobile, dreaming.

12

You go like gypsies. Like popcorn. Watch a grasshopper. They go off, fired from little guns, and land any-old-where. Dragonflies waltz. Kids like you drizzle and spurt. Don't slobber, Violet. Don't make bubbles with your spit. Keep jazzing around, so you don't get bored," Chris said to his daughter.

They waited out Maureen.

13

Maureen grabbed an armrest and pulled herself up. She looked through the back window. The garage doors were open, making a kind of proscenium for the scene outside on the driveway court. There, in hazy evening sunlight, was Chris's car with its broken face.

Maureen groaned and rubbed her eyes. She lifted the door handle. She pushed herself out of the car and snuck into the house through the kitchen entry. By the sinks, a glass pot with a little cold coffee was waiting for the next dishwasher load. She hefted the pot with two hands and drank.

Violet boomed through the door and ran at Maureen's legs.

"What time is it?" Maureen said.

Violet thought.

"Why am I asking her?" Maureen said.

Chris came in. "Good evening, Maureen," he said.

"Yeah," Maureen said.

"Anything you want to say?"

"The rebels are in the palace," she said.

"That's approximately right," Chris said.

Maureen snagged the cigarette that Chris tossed her. She got it lighted on one of the burners. "Don't tell me," she said, exhaling. "Howdy hanged himself on his belt. Lola stuck up a savings and loan. And my father ran away from home."

"One out of three," Chris said.

"Grandpa's gone," Violet said.

"Good," Maureen said.

"Grandpa wanted to go away," Violet said.

"Where?" Maureen said.

"Fort Worth for a while," Chris said. "I think he said L.A. too. He's got some family in Atlanta? He mentioned Atlanta."

"An extended trip," Maureen said. "Well, good. And while he's gone, you're going to be our father?"

"The thing is," Chris said, "he didn't mention oming-cay ack-bay."

"Cut the pig Latin," Maureen said. "I don't hide the ugly truth. He's not coming back?"

"Grandpa isn't?" Violet said.

"Settle down," Maureen said.

"I'm pregnant," Lola said, straying in from the back of the house. She was still in her bathrobe and scuffs. She had a decorator box of tissues under one arm.

"That's nice," Maureen said. "Who was it, Howdy, Dad, or Chris?"

14

Howdy was in the old garage downstairs from his apartment. He'd hung three yellow bug bulbs in a row, and now he stood in the center of the floor with his hands on his hips and his eyes on the cement.

"He lives," Chris said, trotting up.

"Hello," Howdy said.

"Looking at your shoes there?"

"Just looking," Howdy said.

"It's very yellow in here," Chris said. "Did you make it all yellow, Howard?"

"Don't try to be funny," Howdy said. "I'm the funny one, not you. And don't take me for an idiot, either. It's the worst mistake you could make about me. I only let some people take me for an idiot, and you're not one of them."

Chris snapped his head back as though he'd been slugged by a champion.

They went together across the yard and toward the main house. "Daddy left us?" Howdy said.

"This afternoon," Chris said. "Took the Saab out to the airport and somebody's supposed to pick it up."

"He must have been feeling bad," Howdy said. "He never even said good-bye."

"That'll happen," Chris said.

15

Maureen and Violet were playing with a balloon, breathing the helium inside it.

"What's wrong with my voice?" Violet said.

Maureen took the balloon, let loose its opening, and sipped some of the gas.

"The same thing that's wrong with mine," she said, and then she said, "Oh," and moved to the breakfast room windows to gaze out into the yard.

Howdy was on the driveway, kicking up twigs. Chris stood on the grass, his cigarette a dot on his fist. He was looking at the big house.

Lola came over and watched with Maureen.

"Napoleon," Lola said. "Or Magellan."

"Yes," Maureen said. "And either way, it's curtains."

A Note on the Type

The text of this book was set on the Linotype in a type face called Baskerville. The face is a facsimile reproduction of types cast from molds made for John Baskerville (1706–75) from his designs. The punches for the revived Linotype Baskerville were cut under the supervision of the English printer George W. Jones.

John Baskerville's original face was one of the forerunners of the type style known as "modern face" to printers—a "modern" of the period A.D. 1800.

Nonpareil Books

FICTION: 

Hasen
by Reuben Bercovitch
160 pages; $7.95

The Mutual Friend
by Frederick Busch
224 pages; $9.95

The Obscene Bird of Night
by José Donoso
448 pages; $10.95

The Franchiser
by Stanley Elkin
360 pages; $10.95

Searches & Seizures
by Stanley Elkin
320 pages; $10.95

Bear
by Marian Engel
144 pages; $9.95

Desperate Characters
by Paula Fox
176 pages; $8.95

In the Heart of the Heart of the Country *& Other Stories*
by William Gass
240 pages; $9.95

Fairy Tales for Computers
ed. by Leslie George Katz
260 pages; $7.95

The Chateau
by William Maxwell
416 pages; $10.95

The Folded Leaf
by William Maxwell
288 pages; $9.95

Old Man at the Railroad Crossing
by William Maxwell
192 pages; $10.95

Over by the River *& Other Stories*
by William Maxwell
256 pages; $9.95

Time Will Darken It
by William Maxwell
320 pages; $10.95

They Came Like Swallows
by William Maxwell
192 pages; $9.95

Disappearances
by Howard Frank Mosher
272 pages; $10.95

Five Women
by Robert Musil
224 pages; $8.95

Famine
by Liam O'Flaherty
480 pages; $9.95

Days
by Mary Robison
192 pages; $8.95

Oh!
by Mary Robison
224 pages; $9.95

Kindergarten
by Peter Rushforth
208 pages; $9.95

All Sail Set
Armstrong Sperry
192 pages; $8.95

David R. Godine, Publisher
300 Massachusetts Ave.
Boston, Massachusetts 02115

All *Nonpareils* are printed on acid-free paper that will not yellow or deteriorate with age. All are bound in signatures, usually sewn, that will not fall out or disintegrate. They are permanent softcover books, designed for use and intended to last for as long as they are read.